# THE DEAD DON'T FORGIVE

D. C. PICKLO

Copyright © 2024 by D. C. Picklo

All rights reserved.

No part of this publication may be reproduced, distributed, or transmitted in any form or by any means, including photocopying, recording, or other electronic or mechanical methods, without the prior written permission of the publisher, except as permitted by U.S. copyright law. For permission requests, contact business@dcpicklo.com.

The story, all names, characters, and incidents portrayed in this production are fictitious. No identification with actual persons (living or deceased), places, buildings, and products is intended or should be inferred.

ISBN 979-8340636287

Book Cover by Hampton Lamoureux

*For everyone I lost along the way.*

# ONE

THIS NIGHT WAS like any other. I found myself cold and alone, standing in an unfamiliar and unfathomable darkness where anything beyond arm's length was simply enveloped in it like a monumental blanket of despair. I'd usually spend what felt like hours wandering through its empty expanse, searching for a sign of life—a sign that this infinite realm of grief and agony might have a conclusion. How I wished there was meaning to it all.

But something was different about tonight. After my customary voyage within the blackness for an indiscernible amount of time, the shroud seemed to lift away, revealing an all too familiar house—one that I wished I could erase from my mind. Yet it remained daunting. *No, not this place. Anywhere but this place. Please,* I begged to myself, the thoughts in my head racing. As I began to back away from it, there was a loud blast from somewhere just beyond my view, and the house went up in a roar of red flames, the sound of the blaze near deafening. With nothing left to do, I collapsed to the ground, digging my hands into the neatly cut grass beneath me, screaming until I was sure my vocal cords tore. And, then, there was nothing once more.

I awoke to the sound of my bedside alarm beeping incessantly as it did most mornings, the dark red digital interface flashing the time: 5 AM. I quickly switched it off and lay there for a moment, collecting my thoughts in the dark of my room. The curtains before me concealed the early morning light, though it still managed to peak around the edges as though it knew I could not hide from it forever. I sat up and rubbed my eyes until they began to hurt.

*Four hours of sleep last night*, I thought to myself. It was more than I had managed in many months, possibly years, at this point. The room was growing brighter now; not even the curtains could keep the light out much longer. With a great sigh, I tossed aside my blankets and stood, the old floorboards groaning beneath my feet as I made my way to the window. I pulled the curtains aside and unleashed the first light, admitting defeat for another day.

Before me was a view I had never truly gotten sick of seeing: a picturesque valley below with a winding river at its base and a two-lane, asphalt road nestled alongside it that rarely saw travelers. The hillsides were covered in mighty pines that stood over a hundred feet tall. But perhaps the best part of it all, at least to someone of better taste and less predisposed to hiding in the dark, was the brilliant orange and red sky as the sun crested the treetops across the divide.

When I was younger, this sort of view would have brought me to tears just in awe of it. Never in my travels had I seen something quite like it, and I had it all to myself. But that was the catch: I was alone. And it was likely for the best.

After taking in the morning view, I turned to my left and gazed upon the closet door that stood slightly ajar. It was caked in the cheapest white paint money could buy with visible run lines. No doubt the work of the previous owner. It always glistened in the morning light, the poor craftsmanship becoming more apparent and every flaw on full display. I figured that today was the day I'd finally strip the damn thing and paint it properly.

The door groaned as I opened it, protesting. In the dark of the closet, I instinctively reached for the metal chain that dangled in the shadows, giving it a pull. Suddenly, the space was bathed in a warm light from the bulb overhead. I didn't have much in here. I combed my way through a few pairs of jeans and plucked the one with the fewest holes from the rack before turning around and grabbing the first shirt I could see. In one fluid motion, I reached for the metal chain adjacent to the bulb, pulled, and exited the closet, kicking the door shut behind me as I went. I heard the click of the latch as I laid my selection down on the bed.

After getting dressed, I exited my room and into the long, shadowed hallway beyond. There was no natural source of light here, only what crept in from the rooms attached. Directly across from me was my washroom, perhaps the smallest one in existence. I quickly freshened up there before returning to the hallway once again, this time following its length to the set of stairs at its end, passing two other rooms on either side as I went. Both were bedrooms I had not found uses for yet. I descended the single flight of stairs, which brought me into my cramped kitchen. The light of the new day had not yet made it to the back of the house, so shadows engulfed the space.

I worked my way around the four-seat dining room table I had haphazardly placed a mere two feet from the foot of the stairs, careful not to trip over any of the many cardboard boxes strewn about, many of which were still sealed from the move. Maneuvering my way into the kitchen, I stopped before the refrigerator, a monolith of off-white plastic from the early Eighties at best, affixed with metal handles and a vinyl, faux wood panel running their narrow lengths. I opened the freezer door at the top and surveyed what I had in stock. It was a limited selection of frozen vegetables, what appeared to be ground beef that had been there since I moved in, and a number of microwavable burritos.

I grabbed two of the latter, peeling back the plastic shrouds and tossing them on a plate I took from the cabinet to my right. The microwave sat in the opposite corner between the stove and sink, respectively. I opened the door, placed my breakfast within, and set the timer. While it was cooking, I toggled the light switch to the left of the stove, which turned on a few recessed lights in the ceiling above the sink.

The kitchen itself was incredibly dated. The walls were covered in the tackiest floral wallpaper I had ever seen, matching the dark green tiles on the floor, which I could only assume were asbestos. The cabinets themselves were not much better, caked in the same cheap, white paint as my bedroom closet door. Updating this space would likely cost a small fortune.

The microwave alarm went off, and I retrieved my breakfast, eating it where I stood as I leaned against the counter. The first few bites were incredibly hot before becoming ice-cold while also lacking much flavor. After finishing the two burritos, I dropped the plate into the sink alongside all of the other unwashed dishes I had yet to do from yesterday and the day before. I'd get around to them after fixing the door.

By now, the sunlight was beginning to creep its way into the kitchen through the larger entryway by the table. I made my way over to it, stopping briefly beside one of the few opened boxes along the way. It was a stack of leather-bound photo albums, the one at the top already opened to the final page, containing a faded picture of myself and a woman. I quickly closed it, wiping away the tears that had started welling up at the corners of my eyes. Too many bad memories.

Beyond the entryway into the kitchen was the space reserved for a living room, but I am not sure that is what I would've called it in its current, sad state. Surrounded by boxes were a small loveseat, a coffee table, and a television placed on a set of crates. Behind the couch was a large bay window that had its curtains drawn shut, wavering lines of light along its edges. I did not bother opening them up as I made my way to the front door. I put on the pair of worn work boots to the side and grabbed a set of keys from a nail.

I stepped out into the crisp morning air, letting it wash over me as I stood there for a moment to take it all in. I could smell the sweetness of the pine trees in the wisps of the breeze. I felt an inner warmth I had all but forgotten, but it quickly faded as I heard the distant rumble of thunder down the valley. I hurriedly made my way down the front steps, crossing a narrow, covered porch as I went. I could feel the breeze changing around me, the pleasantness having seemingly disappeared as the wind shifted. Now I could smell the coming rain.

Working my way down the gravel walkway toward a dilapidated garage, I felt the first drop of rain catch the back of my head. Rushing for the door to the side of the structure, another clap of thunder let out, this time much closer. I threw it aside and stepped into the garage. Within sat a beat-up truck, the dark blue paint worn after sitting in the sun for many years and dirt stains that would never go away. It looked tired, just like me.

I walked around to the driver's side, unlocked the door, and climbed into the cab. It was a single with only enough room for a passenger, but that was rarely an occurrence for me these days. I typically just kept a box of tools there for ease of access when the truck inevitably broke down. In the cup holder tucked in the driver-side door was a thermos. I pulled it out and gave it a quick shake, the contents sloshing around inside. Opening it up and taking a sip, I realized this was cold, black coffee from the week prior. But it would have to do as I did not want to pay for more when I got to town.

I put the key in the ignition and turned it over, the engine roaring to life. I put it in gear and crept out of the garage. By this point, the storm had made its way up the valley, and the rain was coming down in curtains, almost to the point where the meager wipers couldn't keep the windshield clear. I took it slow down the gravel driveway, the wet stones crunching beneath the tires as I inched along by memory. Once I had reached the tree line again, the downpour was more manageable, and my visibility improved dramatically.

The winding driveway took me down the western slope of the valley from my home upon its hillside, the length of the lane dressed with tall pines and lush undergrowth. I could still hear the crack and rumble of thunder, but it was mostly masked by the pitter-patter of the rain on the cab roof. I turned on the radio and fumbled through a few channels until I found a station that came through somewhat clearly: the local weather and news reports.

"— and it is most certainly going to be a tricky one for them to get out of. On that note, I am handing it over to your favorite area weatherman, Chuck Washburn. What have you got for us this morning, Chuck?" the radio host said, his words hissing between bouts of static.

"Thanks, Todd. As our listeners can attest, we've got a nasty cold front coming through, so no more of that nice sunshine we've had these past few days. We can expect rain for the remainder of the day going into Monday next week. Areas out on the plateau can expect strong thunderstorms with winds up to fifty miles per hour. Down here in the valley, the towns of Ackerman and Wendell can expect some flooding this evening. Today will have a high of fifty-eight degrees and a low of forty-seven. Please check back in for an updated weather report and extended forecast today at 10 AM," Chuck said. The station cut away to a heavily compressed commercial for a local diner in Ackerman with an annoying jingle, forcing me to turn off the radio, leaving the remainder of my drive to the valley floor in silence.

Once I had made it to the road, I took a moment to watch the river before me. What was usually a slow-moving waterway was now a violently frothing rush of brown water barreling down the valley. It was easily up a foot from where it usually rested during calmer weather. This road rarely flooded, but I definitely did not want to stick around in the event that today was the day that tumultuous water would crest the banks and wash the whole road away.

I pulled out to the left, moving against the current to my side, as I made my way upstream toward the small, sleepy town of Ackerman a few miles down the road. I didn't frequent Ackerman all that often, instead keeping to myself as much as I could manage. Wendell was much closer but also somehow even smaller and did not offer much opportunity for purchasing supplies. Unlike its more populous counterpart upstream, Wendell contained a singular gas station, convenience shop, and traffic light, all at the same intersection as you enter the little hamlet. There was a bar I used to find myself at every evening, but I had since quit drinking per recommendations from my doctor.

As I drove, the rain began to let up, coming down as a steady drizzle rather than the downpour it had been earlier. The river to my right still roared away, debris bobbing on its surface. I'd occasionally happen upon a fallen branch that lay in the roadway, but it was nothing my pickup couldn't manage. The road itself was empty of all travelers, but very few in Ackerman had a reason to travel this way, as Wendell was the last settlement up that way before you got into the wilderness. Soon, the areas to either side of the roadway began to widen, and small homes started to crop up. A moment later, a sign appeared reading, "Welcome to Ackerman! Founded in 1898. Population: 987".

The town of Ackerman was nestled on the widest land available on either side of the riverbanks, the relatively steep slopes of the valley towering above on either side. It made the place feel even smaller. Main Street was straddled by two and three-story brick buildings whose exteriors seemed tired and faded. However, the local government had started pushing initiatives to revitalize the area and bring in outdoor tourism, which was reflected in the number of new stores for camping supplies and souvenirs.

After another moment, I found suitable parking between a compact sedan and a large, three-row SUV, both with out-of-state plates. I got out, tossing my thermos into the passenger seat, causing it to bounce off of the tool case I kept there. I winced at the metallic cacophony I had caused, knowing that something was surely dented as a result of my haste. I slammed the solid cab door shut and locked it, placing the key ring into my jacket pocket.

Just as I was preparing to cross the road, a large white truck blew past me, the towing mirrors nearly catching the side of my face. I cupped my hands around my mouth and shouted, "Jackass!" in their wake. I noted the Texan plate and how the damn thing was undoubtedly lifted several inches from stock but looked as though it had never done a day of work in its life. *Typical,* I thought. The behemoth whirled around a corner and was gone from view, swallowed up by a side street. I tossed a quick glance in either direction before continuing across the empty road.

Before me was a squat, white-painted brick building with large, floor-to-ceiling windows affixed to either side of the main entrance. A rusty, dimly lit sign reading "Harvey's Diner" appears overhead. I toyed with the idea of continuing on to my destination a few blocks down the way, but something told me to go inside like there was some significance to Harvey's today, more so than ever before. The rain had started to pick back up again, so I pushed open the dingy glass door, causing a bell hung overhead to jingle as I entered the diner.

The restaurant was nothing special, largely resulting in this only being my second time here. It was long and narrow, the far wall opposite me feeling as though it were a mile away and the side walls being no more than six feet to either side of me. To my left were a series of dated booths that ran the full length of that side, whereas a bar with hightop stools stretched to an enclosed area near the far right corner, presumably the kitchen. There was a shocking amount of dull reds and clouded chrome furnishings strewn about. The only natural light entered the room from the windows at the front of the building.

I found myself in the awkward position of being one of three individual patrons, the other two sitting next to each other about midway down the bar. Just then, a large, burly man exited the backroom, polishing a coffee mug clenched in his brawny hands. We locked eyes for a moment, and he smiled from beneath his thick, dark beard. He nodded to the bar.

"Have a seat wherever ya like. I'll be with you in a moment," he bellowed before putting the mug down in front of one of the other patrons and pouring fresh coffee into it. I could smell its strength from over here, and it made me think about the depressing contents of my thermos sitting in my truck. I selected one of the hightop stools a few seats away from the other two men in the diner, plucking a laminated menu from a condiment holder before me. As expected, it was slick with grease but also very sticky in places.

"Can I get you started with some coffee?"

I jumped a little. Somehow, this man had silently approached and now stood before me, a fresh ceramic mug in one hand and a full pot of dark coffee jostling within. He grinned again, placing the mug on the counter and emptying some of the rich liquid into it.

"Didn't mean to startle ya. First cup's on me."

I nodded my thanks to him, but he lingered.

"Not sure I've seen you before. Traveling from out of town?"

I shook my head, palming the warm ceramic of the mug in my hands, letting the deep flavor of smell penetrate my nostrils. I sighed.

"I've been here once before. I actually live up Route 40, something like ten miles from here. Closer to Wendell than Ackerman."

The man was still smiling, now pouring himself a cup of coffee. He leaned back on the counter behind him.

"Well, welcome back to my diner. I'm sure not much has changed since you were here last," he said with a light chuckle, his eyes seeming to focus on something distant for a second. I took another glance at the menu.

"Could I just get two eggs, scrambled, and a side of bacon?" I asked, returning the syrupy menu to the holder. Harvey nodded, writing it down in the comically small notebook he drew from his apron pocket.

"Coming right up, mister..." he trailed, expectingly.

"Stratton. Sam Stratton."

His smile somehow grew even larger than before. He nodded one more time before walking back to the kitchen. While he was gone, I turned my attention to the box television mounted haphazardly to an arm jutting out of the wall between myself and the other two patrons. On-screen was a weather report containing a radar map of the region, large blotches of red, yellow, and green masked over an aerial representation of the valley.

"We're starting to get early reports that the McCarland River has overflown the embankments near the village of Wendell, and Route 40 has been submerged in places. If you are traveling today, we are strongly advising you to reconsider. The town of Ackerman and surrounding areas are currently under a flash flood warning until one this afternoon. The heavy rain will persist until eleven. Up next: a mother's plea to find her missing son after five days." I looked away from the screen, attempting to tune out the sound.

Shortly thereafter, the door to the kitchen swung open with such force that it struck the wall adjacent. It appeared as though Harvey, whose silhouette blocked the doorway, had kicked it open with the foot he was now actively lowering. He carried three plates, one in each hand and the last upon the crook of his broad left arm, the generous helpings on each platter audibly sizzling even from this distance.

He placed the first two in each hand before the other patrons down the bar, the ceramic clattering on the polished wood surface. The two men immediately dug in as though this was their first meal in days. Harvey meandered his way over to me, letting my plate elegantly slide down his arm and into his hand, a trick he had undoubtedly learned over the course of many years.

"Here ya go, Mr. Stratton," he said as he slid the dish down between my arms on the countertop. The aroma of grease, sweet and smoked bacon permeated my lungs as I was bathed in the rich scents. The food itself was nothing special to behold, just a simple, hardy breakfast, but it reminded me of simpler times. *Maria used to make breakfast like this,* I thought to myself. I could feel tears welling up in my eyes, and I attempted to nonchalantly wipe them away.

"Something the matter, sir?" Harvey asked, the smile disappearing from his face immediately. He began to reach for the plate, perhaps thinking he had delivered the wrong dish. I lifted a hand.

"Absolutely not. This looks wonderful," I said as I coughed, thumping my chest lightly before continuing.

"Could I actually get some more coffee?" I asked, looking up at Harvey and meeting his concerned gaze. He nodded, a small smile appearing once more. He turned around, retrieved the coffee pot from the warmer, and poured more of the liquid into my mug. He placed it before me again.

"Well, just holler if you need anything else. I'll bring the check over when you're wrapping up". I nodded before taking a fork in hand and taking a bite of the scrambled eggs. They were perhaps the fluffiest and richest I had ever had, with a perfect blend of seasonings, likely from the cooktop he uses. Within moments, the plate was spotless, almost as though it was straight out of the dishwasher. Harvey was down by the other patrons, but I could not make out their conversation.

"My compliments to the chef," I called out, symbolically raising my coffee mug into the air as though I were making a toast. The other two men glanced over and did likewise. Harvey was beaming.

"I'll be sure to tell my wife. I'm just the pretty face around here."

The other men chuckled as Harvey pulled away, snatching the check for my meal from near the register as he made his way back over to me. I retrieved my wallet from my back pocket, fetching the sole debit card from within.

"Hope card is okay," I said, handing it to him. He nodded as he gripped it between his fingers.

"Total comes out to five dollars. I'll get this sorted, and we'll get you on your way. Be sure to come back!"

Harvey shuffled his way to the register once more. It was somewhat comedic to watch this behemoth of a man punch in numbers on the device, making it appear almost as if it were some kind of toy you'd give to a young child. Once done, he returned with my receipt and card, handed both to me, and waved as I made my way for the door. After taking a deep breath, I pulled open the door, listening to the bells jangle as I did so, and slipped back out into the rain.

I quickly checked my watch. *Good. Ron's is open now.* I turned to my left and hurriedly walked down the sidewalk, tucking my hands into my jacket pockets and keeping my head down to keep the rain from reaching my eyes. After a minute of trudging through the downpour, I came to an intersection with the main road. I tossed a glance both ways before crossing, the faded white lines of the crosswalk showing the way. Just beyond the other side lay a small parking lot and a brick store. A neon sign on the roof read "Ron's Tool & Hardware Shed" though some of the lettering was dark. It had been like this since I moved here.

I crossed into the mostly vacant lot, stepping over a low cropping of shrubs dividing the asphalt from the sidewalk. Up near the entrance sat the same white pickup truck that had nearly run me over thirty minutes prior, parked diagonally across three parking spots, one of which was clearly marked for handicapped individuals. I shook my head, the water droplets beading at the tips of my hair, shedding onto the ground below.

As I neared the entrance, the automatic doors slid open, revealing the disheveled stock beyond. The floor was littered with seemingly random containers, some marked with pricing, others not, their contents tied together using bungee cable. The store shelves were somewhat more organized, but many items appeared lost, separated from their kind somewhere else in the mess. The aroma inside was an odd mixture of pine and motor oil with a twinge of body odor.

To my right was the main counter, behind which stood a single man. This would've been none other than Ron Suthers. He was of average height and build, perhaps somewhat on the stockier side, donning a pair of dark denim overhauls, a red and black flannel, and a heavily worn baseball cap from a team I did not recognize. His face was grim with narrow features and tired, sunken eyes, a thick, grey beard wrapping around from ear to ear. Before him stood another man, much taller and muscular, with well-groomed, slick-back hair.

"I'm telling you, we do not have that kind of ammunition in stock. You'll have to go back down Route 40 to Pinewood if you need to buy today," Ron grumbled at the other man, seemingly resigned to the argument that appeared to have been ongoing for a while. The other man let out a frustrated sigh.

"Pinewood? That's like an hour away. I'm not driving there in this weather. Can't you just check the back?" the other man scoffed. Ron glared at him.

"I just finished my stock evaluation before you stormed in here. We. Do. Not. Have. Any," he retorted. The man slammed his clenched fist down on the counter. Ron glanced over at me, shaking his head.

"Is that your truck out front?" I inquired. The man whipped around, his eyes piercing me.

"What? Why?" he seethed. I shook my head.

"That's some piss-poor parking. How about you take it down to Pinewood like Ron was saying before the cops notice and tow it to Pinewood for you," I said. His face was turning more red by the second, but then he breathed in deeply, closing his eyes.

"I'll make sure my brother knows about this sorry excuse of a store," he said before pushing past me and out into the rain. His truck roared to life moments later and whipped recklessly out of the parking lot, making a right onto the road toward Pinewood.

"Appreciate the help there, Stratton. That idiot wouldn't take 'no' for an answer," Ron called out as I closed the remaining gap between me and the counter.

"He almost ran me over on Main Street maybe forty minutes ago," I responded, recalling the start the driver had caused me.

"Well, that was about the time I opened today. He was on me as I was unlocking the front door. Said he needed this specific ammunition for a hunting rifle for some camping trip. Not sure what his problem was."

I nodded, feeling that the conversation had run its course. Peeling away, I made my way to the back wall where the painting supplies were, following the signage dangling from the trussed ceiling overhead.

The selection was limited, focusing mostly on whites and earthy tones. I grabbed a small can of paint remover, some sandpaper, a scraping utensil, and a cherry stain. With the items tucked under my arms, I walked back to the counter. Ron was polishing the paint-spattered surface. I placed them down, and Ron began to drag them mindlessly across the scanner, the machine beeping as he did so.

"Doing some housework?" Ron idly queried.

"I'm repainting a closet door," I responded, not looking to make more conversation. Ron persisted.

"How long have you been up the valley now, Stratton? It's been a while now," he pressed.

I nodded. "It'll be two years on Wednesday."

Ron stopped his work, looking up through his bushy eyebrows.

"I know you aren't here looking for advice, but I'm going to give you it anyway. I don't know your story. What you're doing to yourself ain't right. Ackerman's not much, but the people here are kind and welcoming if you give them a chance. It might help whatever battle you're fighting," he spoke in a gruff but sincere way. Ron scanned the last item and placed them all in a thick paper bag. I handed him my card, which he promptly took. No further words were exchanged beyond the pleasantries of a goodbye as I exited the store.

# TWO

I RETURNED to my truck without any further interruptions. It seemed that the heaviest of the rain had subsided, returning to a drizzle as I pulled back into the road, making a U-turn at the nearest intersection. Unsurprisingly, the remainder of the drive back up the valley was lonesome as nobody wanted to brave the elements on a day like today. The river to my left sat just below the embankment, the foaming waves lapping hungrily at its edges.

As I neared my drive, an increasing number of spots where the river had overflown its bed and ventured to higher ground appeared. It was nothing my truck couldn't handle, but I was growing concerned that the road may be washed out ahead. Fortunately, this did not happen as I returned to the gravel path that wound its way up the valley side. I continued in silence all the way up to the top, occasionally disrupted by the dribble of large raindrops crashing over the roof of my cab as they fell from the pine branches.

Once I crested the final rise and my home came into view, I pulled around in a half circle, slipping the truck into reverse as I completed my maneuver. Glancing through my cracked rearview mirror, I backed into the garage, careful to avoid the previous owner's junk still lining either wall. When the curtain of rain pouring down from the overflowing gutters overhead no longer battered my hood, I shifted into park and turned the engine off.

I picked up the thermos from the passenger seat floor mat and dusted it off while examining for the crater I had undoubtedly caused earlier that morning. Sure enough, I found it near the base, but not nearly as bad as I had expected; it could still be used. I tossed it into the paper bag with my painting supplies and heaved it into my arms.

Sheltering it with my body, I hurried from my garage to the front door of my house, fumbling through my jacket pockets for the keys. Once collected, I unlatched the locks and pushed my way inside, the door seemingly resisting for a moment. It took my eyes a while to adjust to the shroud of darkness again. I loosened the frayed laces on my work boots and kicked them to the side, thudding against the door to the basement in the entryway directly across from me. The sound eerily reverberated into the depths beyond.

I moved into the kitchen and up the stairs in the back to the upper level of the house, down the hall to the very end, and back into my bedroom. I placed the brown paper bag, which had unfortunately gotten damp despite my best efforts to shield it, on top of my nightstand. I emptied the contents onto my bed, the metal cans clanking dissonantly.

The door of the closet was already open, so I examined both sides, as well as the latching mechanism and hinges, before remembering I had left my toolbox in the truck. I shut the door and frustratedly made my way back down to the garage to fetch my tools, berating myself as I did so for the hassle. Fortunately, the rain was letting up, and the birds were singing in the trees around me, which brought a momentary smile to my face.

After lugging the cumbersome case back up to my room, I felt off, sending a small chill down the nape of my neck. The closet door had cracked open. I shuffled closer, my heart thumping in my chest, only to be relieved to see that the latch hadn't engaged as it was instead stuck in its metal housing, likely caught on the layers of paint that had been plastered onto it over the years. I laughed at myself for becoming so easily startled by something so trivial.

I spent the next several minutes removing the hinges from the door, careful to keep the surface propped up so that it would not collapse. Once I had completed my task, I leaned the door against the wall adjacent to the closet. From within, I fetched a set of tattered sheets to lay down on the floor for a suitable working area. I cracked open the window to let the outside air circulate within the space.

Reading over the paint remover directions, I quickly realized that this task should not be performed indoors and that the fumes would be dangerous to inhale. I glanced back outside, seeing the rain clouds looming overhead, weighing my options.

"If I don't do this today, I never will," I said to myself, looking down at the can that I held between my hands. I placed it on the window sill, returning to my bed to dig through the contents of the toolbox. After a moment, I found the respirator I had been searching for. Strapping it to my face, I lowered the detached door onto the bed sheets. Breathing in deeply, I popped open the can of paint stripper and doused the surface of the door in the chemicals. Unsurprisingly, I could still smell it from within the respirator, but I carried on nonetheless.

Within a few minutes, the years of caked-on paint

began to peel away from the wood, revealing glimpses of the grain below. I got to work with the scraper, moving in long strokes down the length of the door, the viscous gobs of off-white paint gliding off its surface. The door took maybe another hour to fully clear, but the time seemed to melt away, much like the paint. Underneath was a beautiful mahogany door with swirling, elegant grain patterns. It truly made me question the sanity of anyone who would want to cover this up.

Giving the wood some time to rest before I worked on the stain, I picked myself up off the floor and hobbled out of the room, attempting to straighten out my back after sitting awkwardly for so long. I pulled the respirator down off my nose and mouth, feeling a huge pressure relieved from my face, letting it dangle from my neck. Making a quick trip to the bathroom across the hall, I freshened up and made my way downstairs.

In the kitchen, the early afternoon sun had brightened the room much more than when I had departed this morning. Unfortunately, the light now revealed the mess I had made of the space with my lack of unpacking. Nearly every inch of usable counter space was covered in half-opened boxes, old papers, and various oddities that had yet to find a proper home. I always felt shame coming down here in the day, which is why I tried to avoid it as much as possible.

I worked my way over to the exhausted-looking pantry to the right of the refrigerator, taking stock of what I had. I could feel the hunger setting in with grumblings from my stomach as it protested my lack of food since breakfast at Harvey's several hours prior. I was touched by a twinge of sadness at the thought of my meal again but quickly pushed it out of my mind.

Within the pantry was a handful of chiefly food-barren

shelves with most of the contents mimicking the same inundation of rummage as the rest of the kitchen. From what little food options I did have in stock, I retrieved some store-branded toaster pastries. As if I were an animal, I consumed them where I stood in a matter of moments, perhaps not realizing how hungry I actually was. I topped it off with a bottle of water that had an unpleasant aftertaste, likely the result of sitting out in the sun for too long at one point.

Feeling refreshed, I dropped my refuse in the plastic bin near the pantry, donned my respirator once more, and returned to my work. I rubbed the surface of the door with a spare cloth, removing any flakes of dried paint and any residue from the stripper. I cracked open the can of stain and began delicately applying it to the panel in long, gentle strokes, making sure not to let it grow too thick in any one area. Almost immediately, the glossy veneer drew out the rich texture and depth of the wood beneath. I let the first side dry before repeating the process on the back.

By the time my task had been completed, the sun was hanging low in the sky, peeking out occasionally from the surrounding clouds. I took a moment to examine them, noting that rain was still on the way, but the late afternoon reprieve was acceptable nonetheless. I tossed a glance over my shoulder at the bedside clock, seeing that it was now half past six. Almost as though a switch had been flicked, I felt famished. I reattached the hinges to the door and reinstalled it into the closet doorframe, taking a moment to just appreciate how much better it looked now.

I removed my respirator, tossed it onto the bed, and opened the window some more to allow more air to circulate within the room and hopefully clear out some of the chemical odor that clung to it. I fetched a replacement set of clothes from the closet, testing that the door wouldn't come crashing down. Feeling confident in my work, I took my change of clothing with me to the bathroom, where I took an immaculate, cold shower.

Once cleaned, I shaved some of the longer strands of my beard and mustache. Setting the razor down, I examined myself in the mirror. My long, auburn hair was in desperate need of a cut at a professional salon, mismatched in length and rugged. I attempted to take better care of my facial hair, but I felt I gave the impression of a lumberjack more so than a former insurance salesman.

Despite only being a month beyond thirty-two years old, I looked much older. The creases and lines that accentuated the features on my forehead and mouth gave the impression of someone in their forties. But my eyes were the worst. I looked exhausted. The shadowy bags beneath them seemed almost a permanent feature at this point. I shook my head. *You deserve this*, I thought to myself, sneering.

I finished drying off, tossing the damp towel into the corner near the hamper where I discarded today's clothes, the smell of the diner and paint stripper permeating the air around them. It would be a problem for me to handle tomorrow as I did not have much energy left. Putting on my fresh clothes, I exited the bathroom and made my way back down to the kitchen to prepare a late meal. By now, the sun was starting to set, throwing the house into the shadow of the hillside.

To keep it simple, I decided to heat up some leftovers I had from dinner the day before, an incredibly poor excuse for lasagna. Cooking had never been a strong suit of mine, and this adjustment over the past two years had forced me, in vain, out of my comfort zone. While it warmed in the microwave, I listened the the hum of the appliance and the spluttering of the sauce in the dish. It popped and crackled for a few minutes before I shut it off and pulled the plate out from within.

Fetching a fork from a box placed next to the stove, I made my way into the dark of the living area. I placed them down on the coffee table and retrieved the television remote from the crevices of the loveseat cushions. I flicked it on, illuminating the room in an ominous blue glow. I cycled through a few channels before settling on what appeared to be a black-and-white western. Reaching for my plate of now-cold lasagna, I settled in for the night.

---

I WASN'T sure what time it was when I awoke. I spent a moment fumbling around in the dark, trying to locate the television remote whose counterpart had seemingly shut off some time along the way. Conceding defeat, I stood up, the plate I had forgotten was on my lap, crashing loudly to the floor before shattering into several pieces. I cursed under my breath. Then I heard a muffled thump from somewhere upstairs.

The hairs on the back of my neck stood on end. Something felt wrong. Incredibly, incredibly wrong. Thinking quickly, I moved silently to the entryway into the kitchen. There was another knock from above, perhaps from one of the unoccupied bedrooms, but I couldn't be sure. I glanced around the kitchen, looking for a suitable weapon, my eyes briefly catching the time displayed on the stove: 2 AM.

I snuck over to the box I had gotten my fork from earlier, carefully rummaging through it until I found and unsheathed a hefty meat cleaver. Armed, I made my way over to the stairwell, a much louder thud ringing down from the dark. Creeping up the steps so as to not cause the warped boards to creak beneath my feet, I slowly made my way to the second level, the handle of my weapon clenched tightly in my right hand.

Once in the hallway, I could see light peering out from underneath the first door on the right. I reached for the knob with my sweating, open left hand, the cleaver raised high above my head. Breathing in deeply, I swung the door open.

Inside, the room was nearly empty of clutter compared to the rest of my home, a single, unshaded bulb hung precariously from a cable in the middle of the room, directly over a dusty box. I examined the edges of the room, confirming that there was nobody else there, before entering the rest of the way.

Loosening the white-knuckle grip on the handle of the cleaver, I approached the box. Scrawled on the top was 'Maria'. I collapsed to my knees, weeping, the weapon clattering to the floor as I cupped my face in my hands. After only a few seconds, the light flickered and let out an audible pop before ceasing to work, returning the room to darkness.

Feeling uneasy again, I grabbed the cleaver again and backed to the door. Pulling it aside, I stepped back out into the hallway. Only it was not the same hallway I had entered from. Instead, this space was much different. A plush area rug ran the length, with bright sunlight pouring in from the rooms on either side and a large window at the very end. I could hear the blissful sound of a woman humming somewhere beyond.

*I can't be here*, I thought to myself. I attempted to back up into the room I had just exited, only to find that the door was no longer there, replaced instead by a small stand holding a vase of lilies. Seemingly of its own accord, the vase toppled over, smashing on the hardwood floor below, the water seeping into the adjacent area rug. The humming ceased, in its place now was the sound of screaming.

Almost instantly, flames sprouted from the walls as the hallway was engulfed in a roaring fire. I began to rush from door to door, checking inside each room for the source of the wailing woman. Once I got to the final room, I could hear her clearly on the other side. But the door would not open. She cried out for me, calling my name, but I could not get to her. I could feel the skin on my hands searing as the hungry flames lapped at my flesh. The world around me fell into complete and utter silence for one brief moment as the woman spoke in a calm voice, bordering on a whisper.

"How could you let this happen to me, Sam?"

---

It was then that I jolted awake, the plate of half-eaten lasagna crashing to the floor, my mouth agape in a silent, panting scream. I clutched at my shirt as though it were suffocating me. Collapsing out of the seat and sprawling on the floor, I writhed while gasping for air as my heart raced. After a few seconds of calming myself down, I could take a few shallow breaths, listening to the drone of the television static.

Lifting my left hand after noticing it becoming wet, I examined it in the wash of the screen's blue light. From several small lacerations on my palm, a steady stream of blood seeped. I winced, now realizing I had broken the plate and had thrown myself on the shattered ceramic pieces. Carefully picking myself up from the floor so as to avoid accidentally finding more of the shards, I made my way into the kitchen, clutching my bleeding hand in my shirt to keep the sanguine liquid from staining the carpet any more than it already had.

Over the sink, I felt the wounds, probing for lingering pieces of the plate still tucked under the surface of my skin. Feeling a piece in my palm below my thumb, I breathed in, slowly pinching the skin with my free hand, working the ceramic out of the cut. Once freed, I dropped it into the basin, clinking as it struck the porcelain bottom. I removed a few more before wrapping paper towels around the hand to contain the bleeding while I searched for my first aid kit.

Finding it on the dining room table, I removed the gauze, isopropyl alcohol, and the stitching set. Returning to the sink, I turned on the overhead light to better see what I was doing. I rinsed out the puncture wounds the best that I could and doused them in the sterilizer, wincing before taking in a deep breath and biting down on the collar of my shirt. I made quick work with the needle, patching up the gashes.

Once satisfied, I cut the excess lengths of the sutures and wrapped my hand in gauze. Thankfully, I was able to contain the bleeding. Now that I had a moment, I leaned back on the counter, letting my thoughts drift back to what I had dreamt about. It had been a very long time since I had experienced something as raw as that, perhaps longer than I had been here.

I stumbled up the staircase and down the dark hallway to my bedroom. Closing the closet door as I passed, I retrieved the leather-bound journal I kept on my bedside stand. Turning on the small lamp that sat on top of it, I flipped through the pages until I found a free one. I dated it in the header before jotting down as much as I could recall from the nightmare. Knowing that I could not risk going back to sleep that night, I decided to lie awake there, sprawled atop my sheets until first light a few hours later.

---

The morning that followed was mostly uneventful as I cleaned up the mess I had caused that night. I had to take another shower to clean off all of the dried blood that now clung to my arm and chest. Feeling exhausted, I got dressed as quickly as I could, careful to avoid using my injured hand too much. Clamoring down the stairs and down the gravel walkway to the garage, I climbed into my truck and started down the drive.

I felt as though I were floating during the foggy trip into Ackerman. I pulled into a spot across the road from the Diner, choosing not to attempt parallel parking. Getting out, I glanced both ways before crossing the street, remembering my close encounter the morning before. Pushing my way through the glass door, listening to the bells jingle as I entered, I looked around for Harvey.

As with the day before, he was busy at work behind the counter, this time serving a much larger group. His head shot up, glancing in my direction. I waved my bandaged hand. He made an exaggerated, wincing face and beckoned me over to a seat at the bar, which I promptly obliged. After taking my seat, he rushed over, a mug of steaming coffee already in hand.

"You look like you've had a rough morning. Stick your hand in the garbage disposal?" Harvey asked as he set the cup down in front of me. I nodded.

"I broke a plate," I said, flipping my hand over on the counter so that the palm was facing up. He inspected it briefly as though he was some sort of medical professional.

"It would seem so," he said, smiling. "And here I am thinking you had lost a fight with a table saw."

I grinned slightly, finding his humor amusing. I could tell he was pleasant company, and it was no surprise that he could attract such a crowd this early in the day. I pulled the syrup-glazed menu from the condiment holder, scanning it, before ultimately settling on the same meal as the day before. And, just as with the previous morning, it was sitting on the countering in front of me within moments.

"How handy are you, Harvey?" I asked as I was finishing up my food, feeling an indescribable urge to take charge in my life from seemingly nowhere. Harvey, who had his back turned to me as he was making a new pot of coffee, let out a hearty chuckle.

"Looking for a hand with some housework since you're down one?" he snickered.

I let out a breathy laugh, smiling. "Yeah, I guess you've got me there. Just have some small projects I wanted to get done this weekend that are now substantially harder to do on account of this," I said, waving my bandaged hand around.

"I close up early on Sundays. Bring some beer and I'll be there around five," he declared. I wrote down the address on a loose napkin, which he promptly tucked into his back pocket. I paid for my meal with my card, gulping down the last cup of coffee, and made for the door.

"Make sure you get light. I'm trying to lose weight!" he called out, patting his stomach. I nodded in acknowledgment as I stepped back out into the crisp morning air. Getting back into my truck, I drove down the road, making a right at the intersection near Ron's, which took me over the bridge crossing the river. Immediately on the other side of the overpass was another parking lot, this one being for the general goods store.

I fetched some supplies, collecting a few cases of beer and more frozen foods, before checking out and returning to my truck. From there, I made the long drive back to my home, where I restocked my freezer and pantry before cleaning up what remained of the lasagna stains in the living room from last night. After all was done, I patiently waited for Harvey's arrival in the dark.

---

I HEARD Harvey's bike thunder its way up my gravel driveway sometime shortly after five-thirty. He parked it under the overhang in front of my garage, hurrying his way up my front steps. Before he had a chance to try out my doorbell, I welcomed him inside, dropping an ice-cold beer into his large hand. He looked around, taking in the entryway and living room, nodding to himself.

"Not what I was expecting. Thought I'd see more artwork or something like you were a reclusive dealer in fine pieces from the Old World. But I'm not one to speak. I live in a one-bedroom apartment with a mattress on the floor," he chuckled, cracking open the beer can, "So what kind of work do you need a hand with?"

"Right now, just moving some things from one room to another, possibly throwing some trash out. We'll probably be tearing up old carpet as well, but we'll see how far we get with the other stuff first. There's a lot of it," I responded, beckoning him to follow me upstairs. I led him to the room I had visited in my dream the night before, bringing him inside. Flipping the switch beside the door, the room was illuminated, light dancing off of the dust particles that hung in the still air.

Much like the kitchen and living room, boxes towered to the ceiling along the walls. Most of it was trash that could very likely be thrown away, and I would never miss nor remember the contents lost, but I had to find the box from the night before. I motioned to the mess around me.

"We'll just move these across the hall. Feel free to grab more beer from the refrigerator downstairs if you run out. And, if you find a box with 'Maria' written on the top of it, let me know. I'll want to go through that one."

Harvey acknowledged, immediately turning to the closest stack of cardboard. We worked for several hours and through a whole case of beer before we found what I was looking for.

---

"Hey, Sam. I think I found that box," Harvey called out from the corner he had been working in. I set down the stack of photo books I had been sifting through to make my way over to him, looking down over his shoulder. The box he was hunched over was identical to the one I had seen in my dream, though much more dirty, years of neglect having caught up with it. I swooped in and pulled it away, a cloud of dust rushing off its surface, making the both of us cough. With my one good hand, I pulled the top open, revealing the contents.

It was a mixture of things: some clothes, tarnishing jewelry, and a stack of sooty picture frames. I pulled the first one from the top, brushing off the surface with my thumb. The image beneath was of my younger self, smiling widely, carrying a beautiful brunette woman in my arms. Her long, flowing hair hung down, the tips almost touching the ground. We were both happy. By now, Harvey had shifted, squatting down next to me.

"Someone important?" he asked solemnly. I brushed a tear from my eye, nodding.

"She was everything."

Harvey placed a heavy hand on my shoulder while staying silent.

"What happened, if you don't mind my asking?" he queried after a moment.

"This was taken shortly after our fifth wedding anniversary. She died in a house fire two weeks later. We were renting this place on the coast to celebrate. I left the gas on on the stove and didn't notice until something must've sparked. Took out the whole kitchen. The firemen found me unconscious in the yard when they arrived. Said I was lucky to have survived..." My trembling voice trailed off. I rubbed my eyes before continuing.

"They couldn't find her in time. The house eventually collapsed. Found out later that killed one of the firemen, a boy no older than nineteen, working alongside his father. I... I killed them both." I dropped my hands into my lap, the picture frame sliding from my palms and onto the floor. Harvey squeezed on my shoulder.

"I didn't know. I'm sorry to make you relive that, but it really doesn't sound like your fault, man."

I shrugged off his hand. Harvey stood up, walking slowly to the only window in the room. The shadows were growing long now, indicative of the setting sun. With his back turned to me and arms thoughtfully crossed, he began to speak.

"I used to work for a shipping company out in Michigan. Made many voyages on those lakes, just like my father before me. He died when I was sixteen. Went down with the Edmund Fitzgerald in seventy-five. My mother begged me to stop, but she was disabled and couldn't work, and I was uneducated and had to keep the lights on for us. One night, when I was about twenty-six, we have these storms blowing in from the west. Massive swells out on the water, maybe ten-fifteen feet tall, but it was nothing we hadn't handled before." He paused, his voice catching in his throat.

"We had brought aboard a boy as a deckhand. Said he was eighteen on his papers, but everybody knew he was younger. Same background as me. Dad was gone, and he needed to be the man of the house for his mom and siblings. I knew he wasn't old enough, but signed off on his papers anyway, thinking I was helping the young lad out. It was his first time out on the open waters of Superior. I called him below deck when the waves got bad, but he stayed on deck, trying to keep the cargo tied down. I didn't notice he disobeyed my orders until the storm was at its worst. I scoured that ship. Every damn nook I could think of while the waves and rain poured down overhead. Eventually, the captain ordered me down, saying that there was nothing more I could've done. We radioed the coast guard, but they were never able to find his body. I still call his mother every Sunday to check in on her and her family." He turned around to face me, his eyes and cheeks red, brushing them off with his sleeve.

"But I don't blame myself for what happened. I did everything I could've, but sometimes life just sucks, and nothing you ever do will be enough to change that. You need to forgive yourself. I'm sure she would've wanted you to, just like this boy's mother said to me." Harvey held out his brawny hand, which I took, hoisting me up from the floor. I sighed, surveying the now half-empty room.

"How about some more beer? I can put a frozen pizza in the oven if you're hungry," I said. Harvey smiled at me and nodded. We both made our way downstairs for a bite to eat and some more beverages before spending several more hours clearing out the rest of the room. Satisfied with our work, I invited Harvey to stay, offering the couch in the living room, which he was obliged, having had perhaps too many beers. I retired to my room, pondering what he had said to me as I drifted off to sleep.

---

I AWOKE to find myself outside, in the rain, standing on a grassy knoll that overlooked a dreary cemetery. A crowd in black had gathered near a gravesite below. I hesitantly made my way down to them. As I got closer, the congregation evaporated into a cloud of smoke that was carried away in the wind, leaving in their wake only one individual, hunched over the freshly-turned soil, whimpering.

When I got within a few feet of him, the man looked up, staring directly into me with a burning fury. It was me. He rose, hands clenched in fists as he approached, stomping the mud beneath his shoes so that it coated his suit's pant legs.

"You did this to me! You killed her!" he shouted, pointing a finger at me as he drew closer. I attempted to back away, but it was too late. He was on me within seconds, forcing me to the ground and pummeling my face and body with a flurry of punches that carried an immense weight beyond that of a human. His shouting became distorted and echoed in the wind around us.

After a few minutes, the world fell completely silent.

Composing himself, he stood up, fixing his coat and tie while looking down on me with utter contempt. I attempted to stand up, but he gave me a solid kick to the diaphragm, knocking the wind out of my lungs and causing me to reel backward and tumble into an open grave. Unable to move, I realized I was now stuck in a coffin, the lid precariously lifted to my side.

His silhouette loomed at the foot of the hole. I could feel his gaze piercing me as I lay there. Then, from the silence I had been consumed by, the sickly sweet sound of humming arose from the distance, and a woman in a veiled wedding dress appeared next to him, her head cocked to the side. At that moment, the hum faltered, and the lid of the coffin slammed shut on top of me, locking me in total darkness. Alone.

# THREE

I jolted awake, panting, just like the night before, my body and sheets soaked with sweat. I spent the next several moments trying to regulate my gasps for air, getting my heartbeat back to an acceptable level. Once I was breathing again, I laid back down, deciding it was not worth it to check my clock for the time as it was still dark out. Through the window before me, I could see the moon dancing in and out of view, wispy tendrils of clouds passing in front of it.

I got up, sliding my feet into a pair of worn slippers I kept at my bedside, and worked my way around the bed and out into the dark hallway. Feeling as though I was being watched, I looked down its length toward the stairwell and into a seemingly impenetrable wall of darkness and silence. I looked down at the digital watch I kept on my wrist, pressing down on the crown to activate a backlight: 9:17 AM. My heart sank.

Then, from within the shadow of the stairwell, I heard the creak of a floorboard. The air around me became ice-cold as the hairs on the nape of my neck and arms stood up.

I slowly returned my gaze to the darkness, clenching my teeth. At first, I saw nothing, letting myself grow cautiously optimistic that it was just the temperature change that resulted in the old wooden boards to shift. But then I saw the outline of a face halfway blocked by the top of the stairs.

I spent what felt like several agonizing hours taking in its features despite there being very little I could make out as it was heavily obscured by the shadows. Its visage was gray and gaunt, much like that of a corpse, as though there wasn't enough skin to stretch over the bone. Thin strands of dark hair framed the face, the length running into the darkness and being impossible to discern. But the eyes were the part that haunted me the most.

They were cold and lifeless, sunken deep into the skull, almost to the point where one might have never noticed they were there. They glinted ever so slightly in what little moonlight entered the space, but they were a dull, translucent grey that lacked the same depth of those found on a living person. They were fixed on me as though they were waiting for me to move.

Finally breaking myself free of the horror that held me in place, I slowly started to creep backward into my room, placing a hand on the door so that I could close it and hide from this thing. As I did so, it began to move, creeping further up the stairs. Feeling the fear tingling its way up my arms and legs, I jump back, letting out a small whimper. Within seconds, I could hear it scraping its way down the hallway, just out of view, moving at a speed I didn't think would be possible for something so frail. I did not see it approach as I slammed the door shut, its body colliding loudly with the panel, the hinges buckling from the surprising force.

And then there was nothing. I engaged the lock on the

latch before pressing my ear against the wood, listening. I could not hear it breathing, though I could feel its presence in the void beyond. After a moment, it let out a deep, guttural sound, clicking its teeth. Clamoring back onto my bed, I curled up as tightly as I could, closing my eyes, and tried to calm myself down.

I could still hear it pacing in the hallway, perhaps trying to find another way or try and break its way in. The door wouldn't be able to take another blow like that. Then, from a distance, I could hear what sounded like my bedside alarm clock, muffled. Over the seconds, it grew louder and more clear. The creature beyond my door let out another sound, this time what seemed like one of desperation or frustration.

---

When I opened my eyes again, I found myself in the same position I had been in fear but was surrounded by early morning light and the welcoming sound of my alarm blaring just a few feet away. I quickly looked over at my bedroom door, which was ajar. I shot to my feet, looking over the hinges. After a moment of examination, I realized that they were just as they should be.

Turning off my alarm and letting myself rest, attempting to relax my tensed muscles, I flipped through my journal to make a new entry detailing the experiences I had that night. Never had I had such vivid and terrifying visions, especially not in two back-to-back days. After I was satisfied with my documentation, I got dressed, placing the journal under the crook of my arm as I went downstairs.

To my surprise, Harvey was nowhere to be found. In his place on the couch was a sloppily written note explaining that he had to leave before I got up to get ready at the diner with his wife. I made a note to swing by again this morning to thank him for his help the previous night. Checking the time again, I hurried to my truck to make the long drive out to Pinewood.

---

It was odd to drive through Ackerman without stopping as I rarely ventured beyond its furthest boundaries, only making the trek once a month. The roads past its limits wound their way along the river, which gradually narrowed. Along the route, I'd pass through more settlements that grew larger than the last as I crept my way back into civilization. Soon, the road broke off into a limited-access highway, allowing for more lanes to handle the increased traffic, specifically from all of the logging trucks along this shipping corridor.

Cresting an incline, I found myself overlooking the small, sleepy city of Pinewood, nestled in the valley below, cloaked in a thick, rolling mist. It was much larger than Ackerman, acting as the regional economic hub and the seat of the county government. I never bothered looking into the actual population statistics as they were not conveniently supplied on a roadside sign like Ackerman, but I would've guessed it sat somewhere in the low to mid-twenty-thousand range, easily containing more than a third of the total county population, perhaps even more.

I took the first available exit on my right as I descended into the valley, finding myself on a separated, multi-lane avenue lined with narrow fruit trees. I proceeded down the way for some time, never coming across more than a handful of other cars at any given moment. It was perhaps one of the larger benefits of coming into the city so early on a Monday morning.

After a few more minutes, I made another right turn, pulling into a parking lot before a three-story, brick facade building that was part of a much larger office complex. Many of the windows were dark, signifying that very few people had yet arrived to start their workday, so I had the pick of the parking spots in the lot. After finding a suitable location, I tossed the truck into park and got out.

The air here was not nearly as fresh and welcoming as further up the valley, especially not compared to my home. Even this early, I could smell the fumes from car exhaust and the pungent stink of the Pinewood paper mill several miles away. While having access to the amenities and services a larger settlement provided could even out some of these negatives, it also came with the drawback of more people. I had been to large cities before that would've dwarfed Pinewood, even spending much of my early career in one, but there was no humanity there. Thousands of faces, but no one was really alive. I had hated it after the charm wore off.

After a minute to myself, another car pulled into the lot, a black sedan that was very clearly the latest model for that year. The driver parked a few spots down from me before getting out. He was older but built well with broad shoulders and strong arms, dressed in a golf shirt and beige slacks. He kept his greying hair and beard shaved close to his skin but still long enough to give his face extra definition. He waved at me, the keys to his car dangling in his hand.

"Beat me in this morning? Bet the drive was nice," the man said.

"Didn't get much sleep. Besides, there is less traffic on the roads when I leave earlier," I responded amicably. He smiled before motioning for me to follow him as he unlocked the glass door into the building entryway. We slowly ascended the grand stairwell in the foyer, the elegant craftsmanship and detail from a time that has long since passed, eluding to the age of the building as a whole.

After reaching the top level, we continued down a musty-smelling hallway lined with windowed doors, all of which had their blinds pulled down. Near the end of the corridor, the man stopped and unlocked one of these doors, leading us into a small, windowless waiting area with enough seating for six. Closing the door behind us, he took off his jacket and hung it on a rack in the space.

"Our appointment isn't for another twenty minutes. Let me get everything warmed up and do some prep work, and we can get started early. I'll call you in in a few," he said cheerfully. I took a seat, resting my head against the cool plaster wall, shutting my tired eyes to rest. But all I could see was the creature from my dream staring through me. And just as he had promised, the man called me into the back a few moments later, freeing me from the clutches of its haunting gaze.

The next room was small, with bookshelves that towered all the way up to the vaulted ceilings. There was a leather chaise on the far wall across from an elegant mahogany desk, behind which sat the man in a somewhat comically oversized, plush chair that would've easily fit into a villain's lair in a movie. I took a seat on the chaise, sinking into its chilling embrace as I lay down.

"How are things, Samuel?" the man asked, an old-school pen in his hand, which he gently dipped into the inkwell on his desk.

"I'll be honest, Doctor Abernathy, I am not doing well. I brought my journal, as discussed the last time, to go over together," I responded, gazing up at the beautifully-tinned ceiling above. He jotted something down in his notes.

"Now, Samuel, we've had this song and dance for almost two years now. You can call me by my first name. I may be your doctor, but I am also a friend. And friends open up to each other. Can you tell me more about what you've been writing down?"

"Yes, Harlan. Now, for the last month, I haven't had too much to write about. I made entries for nearly every day since our last session, but most were pretty uneventful. The usual 'today was bad, and I am sad' sort of things right up until two nights ago." I paused, taking in a deep breath and letting Harlan finish what he was writing.

"I started having these dreams—nightmares, really. I don't really know how to describe them beyond what I wrote down, and even then, I don't think they do how I felt justice. I was terrified," I expressed. Harlan set his pen down and stood up, approaching me, a look of concern on his darkening face.

"It isn't unheard of to process grief and remorse in your dreams, but this is a pretty sudden change that I have not seen before. Have you changed anything about your routine? Are you coming in contact with something new that may impact your mental state? New prescriptions or substances?"

I shook my head, frowning. Harlan pondered for a moment, tapping his chin with his index finger.

"What did you dream about?" he queried, returning to his desk.

"Well, the first night was really strange. I fell asleep in my living room..." I started before Harlan interjected.

"Why were you sleeping in your living room?"

"I had used paint remover and stain on a door in my

bedroom and figured sleeping there might not be good for my health. The room hadn't properly aired out by the time the night rolled around."

He recorded something in his notes before signaling for me to continue.

"When I woke up... well... when I thought I woke up, I was still there, but something just felt wrong. You know? I heard this thumping sound from upstairs, so I went to investigate. It was from one of the rooms I was storing a bunch of boxes in, but everything was gone except for this one with Maria's things. Then I was in the hallway of this different house, but it was on fire, and I could hear her calling out to me. Begging for my help, but I couldn't get to her. Then I woke up."

"Okay. And what of this other night?" Harlan looked deep in thought, his brow furrowed.

"This was actually last night. I had an acquaintance over to do some housework because I injured my hand on a broken plate the night before. This other dream had me in the cemetery where we had Maria's funeral, but it was different. And there was another version of me there, but he attacked me, blaming me for what had happened to her. Then I thought I woke up from that, but it was another dream." I could hear Harlan's pen working feverishly.

"This other dream was the one that really shook me up. I felt as though I was awake and was getting up in the middle of the night to use the bathroom, but it wasn't the middle of the night. My watch said that it was nine in the morning."

"Could it have just been that you misread the watch or that it was wrong? Your brain was likely not fully awake," Harlan pressed. I shook my head, though I began to question the events from that dream.

"No... No. I don't think so. I felt fully awake at the time. But when I went into the hallway from my bedroom, there was this corpse-like figure out there at the end of my hallway, watching me in the dark. I could barely make it out, but it was the most terrifying thing I have ever seen. I think it wanted to attack me, but I locked it out of my room until my alarm went off and I woke up," I finished. Harlan put his pen down in the inkwell and adjusted his glasses.

"Samuel, I don't mean to discount this event, but this sounds an awful lot like you were awake, and you just thought you saw something that wasn't really there. A sleep-deprived brain will play tricks on the eyes, and looking at you right now, I can tell you have not been sleeping any better since our last session."

I tried to jump in to defend myself, but he continued.

"As for the first night, it seems like it might just be a combination of the chemical fumes having an effect on your brain. Tell me, did you eat anything before you fell asleep?" he asked. Taken somewhat aback, I let my mouth hang open.

"Yeah, I had some leftovers that I guess I fell asleep while eating. That was the plate I broke and cut up my hand with," I responded, trailing off as I began to doubt the events of the last two nights. Harlan smiled.

"That's very important information there. Indigestion can have some interesting effects on our sleep. Remember Scrooge commenting on how he thought the Christmas spirits might be from some undigested food? This sort of thing can be explained in a similar way. It is totally normal," he said, seeming somewhat pleased with himself for having solved the case in his mind. I wasn't as convinced, but he was making a valid argument.

"So you think that this was just a fluke and that there

were other factors that contributed to these dreams?" I asked. Harlan shook his head in agreement.

"Yes. I think it might just be a combination of your lack of sleep, your choice of meal before falling asleep, and the influence of the grief you are processing. I'll be honest; you had me a little concerned at first that you might be taking illicit substances that might've been contributing to these... happenings," he said as he appeared to finish his note-taking, closing the binder he had been working in.

"I am also happy to hear that you are reaching out to other people in your community. While it is sometimes instinct to process these emotions on your own and shut out others, doing the opposite will have a more positive impact on your path to healing. We are social creatures, and isolation can do some pretty nasty things to the body and mind." He turned, his oversized chair groaning as he did so, and began rummaging through one of his desk drawers. He retrieved a piece of paper, which he promptly stood up and handed to me, leaning over his workspace.

"Seeing that we are making some progress here, I would like to invite you on a little trip I've done every year for the past decade. It's a ten-day hike up through the reserve just north of the town of Wendell. That outlines a lot of it, like what to bring and prepare for, but it's always been a glowing success. I always like to say that a little nature therapy goes a long way. We're heading out next week if you are interested."

I glanced over the sheet before handing it back to him. "I'll be honest. This really isn't something that I want to do right now. Maybe next year, though."

Harlan nodded, but I could see he was disappointed. He sat back down, returning the paper to his drawer.

"Was there anything else you wanted to go over today?"

I LEFT Harlan's office an hour or so later, feeling a little better about myself and the events that had transpired in my sleep. After climbing back into my truck, I made the long drive back up to Ackerman, deciding that I should swing by Harvey's Diner on the way to see him. I don't know that sharing everything I had been experiencing would be best, but he seemed to be well-acquainted with grief and understood me more than my psychiatrist seemed to.

I followed the way I had come into Pinewood, driving back up the valley, the sun now fully over the ridge line to my left. Patches of blue sky peeked through the clouds overhead, but I knew it would not last for long as the radio weatherman confirmed that more rain was on the way. And, sure enough, thirty minutes into the drive, the downpour began.

Pulling into Ackerman, I found a parking spot in Ron's lot, seeing that the main street was filled to the brim already. I hurriedly walked over to the diner, getting drenched in the process. Rushing inside, I took off my jacket, causing it to drip profusely on the welcome mat, my shoes squelching as I walked to an empty hook on the coat rack to hang it from.

The diner was packed this morning; nearly every spot at the bar was filled, and most booths were as well. Seeing that my options were limited, I took a spot at the nearest open table. I noticed Harvey's large figure near the back of the space, taking the orders of a young family. It appeared that there were other workers here today, with one of the young gentlemen coming over to take my request.

I placed my order, a little disappointed that I might not get to speak with Harvey. As the waiter was leaving, I asked if he could mention that I'd like to speak with him. He nodded hesitantly before heading for the kitchen. After some time, much longer than usual, Harvey barreled out of the back, several platters balanced on his arms and hands. He delivered them to their respective tables, chatting with each person he encountered, his face absolutely beaming. I could tell he loved this job, even if it would get hectic like it appeared today.

He arrived at my table last, flagging down a member of the waitstaff as he did so, saying something to them before patting them on the back. Harvey let out a hardy chuckle as he set the plate down before me, the food still sizzling hot from the stovetop. He sat in the seat opposite me, leaning the chair back onto its rear legs.

"Third day in a row. I've known some of these people for years, and I only see them maybe once or twice a week before I think they get sick of me!" he bellowed. I smiled, taking a sip of the coffee. It was not as good today, but it would get the job done.

"Sorry I had to dip as early as I did. We've only got the one set of keys to get into the diner, and I had them with me. Hopefully, I didn't wake you up as I left! By the way, how are you feeling? It was a pretty heavy night."

I set the mug down. "No worries. My alarm woke me up probably a few hours after you left. I'm doing okay, all things considered. Just got back from Pinewood and decided to swing by to thank you for your help," I responded. He grinned.

"Listen, I don't have much time. We're a little short-staffed today, so I gotta get back to the kitchen in a minute. Just had to ask, what sent you out to Pinewood? Never heard you talk about that place before. Hope you're not planning on moving down there!"

"I see a psychiatrist there. Never go otherwise."

Realization dawned on Harvey's face.

"I head there for that too. Glad you're working on yourself. Who's your doc, if you don't mind my asking? Might be able to make a recommendation if things ain't working out," he pressed. Despite the rather forward and personal question, there was just something about him I felt comfortable with.

"I see Dr. Abernathy. He's been pretty good to me, I guess. Not looking for anything different right now, though," I said. Harvey slapped a hand on his knee, the clap ringing out.

"No kidding! He's mine as well. Listen, reason I mention it in such a roundabout way is that he's doing this, like, outdoor hike-retreat thing here next week, and you mentioning Pinewood reminded me. I went last year with the wife, but we just found out she's pregnant, so I'm going by myself this time. I'm sure he's invited you, but I think you should tag along. I've got plenty of gear already, so all you'd need to do is join! It's a good time and really gets your mind off of things. I'm sure you'd like it."

Harvey seemed incredibly excited about this, perhaps the most I had seen him in the limited time we've interacted. I still had my doubts, but I was finding it incredibly hard to turn him down. I took another sip of the coffee, nodding a few times as I did so, forcing myself to concede. I knew that, deep down, this would very likely help me in the end and that I had spent far too long hiding in my own shame.

He leaped to his feet, clapping his thundering hands once. I could tell I had just made his day, and for perhaps the first time in the duration of my stay here, I felt better about myself; I felt a twinge of optimism, even if it would only be fleeting. He thanked me for joining.

"Before you head back, just wanted to let you know that there is plenty more beer and a lot more stuff to do at my place if you've got any free nights in the next week," I called out as he departed. He turned back and gave me a thumbs-up before dipping back into the kitchen.

## FOUR

I stirred shortly after first light, reaching over to reset my alarm before it had a chance to go off. The chilling, summer morning air drifted into my room through the open window, embracing me in the sweet aroma of the dew-dappled pines. I felt invigorated for the day that lay ahead of me.

Sliding out of bed, I hurried over to the closet, shutting the window as I did so. I made one final pass of my remaining clothes before making my selection: a pair of work jeans, a loose, light, and breathable shirt, and a lined flannel for if I got too cold. Throwing these on, I closed the closet door behind me and slung the near-overflowing rucksack I had finished filling the night before over my shoulder.

Adjusting to its weight, I made for the hallway, down the stairs, and into the kitchen, where I quickly ate. During the commotion I was causing, a lethargic Harvey stumbled his way into the dining area, rubbing his eyes as he tried adjusting to the harsh, fluorescent light overhead. He let out a massive yawn, stretching as he did so.

"You're up early," he commented drowsily. I, already mid-bite on a room-temperature microwave burrito, nodded while smirking.

"We've got to meet the group in an hour. The park entrance is fifteen minutes away. You are more than welcome to catch up if you want to head in by yourself," I responded jokingly. He, conceding, buried his head in his hands before dragging them up and through his ragged hair, flattening it against his skull.

"This is the last time I will sleep on that damn couch. Your next project should be setting up a guest room and bed," he exclaimed, pointing his thumb out into the living room.

"I'm going to take a shower, and then I'll be ready," he added as he staggered up the stairs, bouncing off the walls as he ascended. I listened until I heard the door shut and the sound of the water turning on. I stood up, cleaning off my plate of scraps before returning to the freezer to warm up one last burrito, figuring that Harvey probably hadn't eaten anything yet, and I did not want him passing out immediately.

When he had finished freshening up, we met at the front door. He was wearing what appeared to be more in line with the outfit of a fisherman than a hiker, but I found no sense in commenting on it. At least he was wearing proper boots for the occasion. Over his back, he carried several packs, likely a combination of his own supplies as well as our shared equipment. Seeing as he was much larger than I, I would not protest him carrying everything.

As we stepped outside, I handed him the burrito I had prepared for him, wrapped loosely in a paper towel, which had now grown somewhat soggy. He smiled and thanked me, taking a bite. After locking up, we sauntered down to the garage, where we dumped our packs into the truck bed. We climbed into the cab, Harvey shifting my toolbox into the middle seat.

"Don't forget, my bike is out there," Harvey stated as I turned the ignition over, the old engine roaring to life once more.

"Yeah, I'd rather not have that deathtrap scratch my paint," I returned. He looked over at me and snorted.

"What paint? This rust bucket ain't got no paint left," he chortled. I laughed at that one, mostly because he was right. I pulled out, missing his motorcycle parked under the overhang by a foot or so, and began the cruise down my winding, gravel driveway toward the valley floor. Somehow, Harvey had already finished his burrito, seemingly having inhaled it between the front porch and depositing our luggage in the back of the truck.

During the drive to Wendell, I thought about the past week. He had been over nearly every evening after closing up the diner to assist me with some of my projects. With his help, I was able to clear out one bedroom and finally tame the living room. Heeding his advice, I think my next arrangement was going to be setting up a place for guests. I'd love for him and his wife to have a place to stay should they come for a longer visit.

As we approached the village, I pulled off into the lot of the sole gas station, topping off on fuel. From there, we pulled back onto the main road, conveniently just as the singular traffic light signaled us through the intersection. We drove past a few dilapidated structures, the bar I used to frequent, and some homes as we wound our way up the final stretch of Route 40.

Somewhere along the way, the painted lines fell off, and the pavement switched to a material much coarser and rugged than traditional asphalt but still not quite gravel. Shortly thereafter, the road dropped off, transitioning to dirt. The truck rattled, the tires kicking up the stones in the road as they pinged off the metal body. Harvey cranked his window down, peering his head over the edge.

"Sam. I think that rock just took the last of your precious paint."

As he pulled himself back into the cab fully, we rounded a bend in the road, bringing a large, earthy lot into view. There were a few other vehicles parked near the far end of the clearing, a group of people huddled together around an individual holding a large map.

I pulled up alongside the vehicle at the very end of the row, the same black sedan Harlan drove. We leaped down, kicking up more dust as we fetched our gear from the truck bed. It was coated in dirt, which we attempted to brush off to little avail. Admitting defeat, we walked over to the group. The man with the map, who was undoubtedly Harlan himself, turned around at the sound of footsteps, peering up from below the brim of his white bucket hat.

"Welcome, boys! Glad you could make it, especially you, Sam! Was beginning to think we'd be missing you," he exclaimed, reaching out to shake both of our hands. I looked over the faces of the other members of the party, though I did not recognize any of them. Excluding Harlan, there were three others: a short, oblong man who appeared to be in his forties at least, another who was much lankier, with a long, flowing beard, whose age was difficult to discern, and finally, a woman who stood somewhere between their heights with dark hair done up in a messy ponytail.

"This the whole crew, doc? Looks like a lot smaller crowd this year," Harvey asked Harlan. He shook his head.

"Unfortunately, we are still waiting on two more. The

others that typically joined are away for a wedding this year," he responded, not looking up from his map. As if by announcement, another vehicle accelerated around the bend in the road, whipping dirt and rock into the air as it barreled into the clearing. It was the same white pickup that had nearly run me over the week prior.

It pulled up to the left of my vehicle, dwarfing it. The two passengers exited the truck, the driver being the same man I had the unfortunate interaction with at Ron's, a rifle slung over his shoulder, and a duffle bag on the other. He was accompanied by another, older man who he appeared to be related to, perhaps as a brother. As they got closer, I realized he was none other than the local weatherman—Chuck Washburn—whose pictures I had seen from time to time in the newspapers.

Both men looked and dressed eerily similar, donning jeans, white shirts, and baseball caps. Chuck maintained his well-groomed appearance, with a mannered beard and mustache that he undoubtedly primmed every morning. The younger man appeared much the same as when I had the misfortune of seeing him last, with muscular arms that were too large for this shirt and slick-back hair, a pair of jet-black sunglasses resting on the bridge of his nose. It seemed as though he recognized me almost immediately, smirking as he drew closer.

"Hey, if it isn't the guy who threatened me at that damn tool store I was telling you about Chucky," he taunted loudly while nudging his brother with his elbow. Chuck lowered his head, shaking it and muttering something under his breath that I could not pick up. I clenched my fist in my pocket, grinding my teeth in my mouth. Harlan stepped in between all of us and the approaching men, seemingly attempting to defuse the situation.

"Just in time. We were about to head out. Glad you could make it, Chuck and..." Harlan started, reaching out a hand to the human equivalent of smoking cigarettes in a hospital nursery. He arrogantly pushed the doctor's hand aside while drawing closer to me.

"That's my younger brother, Jakob," Chuck said with a sigh, shaking Harlan's hand before closing in on his sibling.

"Jakob!" Chuck shouted, grabbing him by the shoulder and jerking him off of his warpath, "I am not about to have you picking a fight with every person here. I did not tell Ma to send you up here just so you could cause trouble like you do back home." He nodded at me, mouthing "Sorry" as he pulled his seething brother away.

While Chuck attempted to calm his raging brother down, Harlan gathered us all around him. He knelt down, spreading his map out over the dirt and resting a few tools at each corner to keep it from curling back up. He pointed near the bottom left, tapping.

"We're right here. Just outside of the village of Wendell. Over the course of the next ten days, we will work our way further downstream before breaking away up to the north, summiting this mountain right here. Most of this will be off the trails, but I got clearance from the Rangers. Won't be repeating last year's debacle."

A few members of the group, including Harvey, let out a stifled laugh, apparently finding something amusing in a past occurrence I was not privy to.

"Anyone know the name or significance of this mountain?" Harlan asked, looking up at us through his spectacles.

"That's an old volcano, isn't it?" the short man questioned. The doctor nodded.

"Yes. About one hundred thousand years old. Not incredibly old by geological standards, but it has been dormant for as long as we've been here. Many would argue that it is currently dead. Now, early settlers named it 'the Crag' on account of its isolation from other mountain ranges and its difficult-to-traverse rock face. I don't plan on taking us up, but we'll loop around it before making our way back," he finished before folding the map back up and tucking it into his breast pocket.

"Any questions?"

Everyone sheepishly shook their heads as though the sudden realization of what they had signed themselves up for had sunk in. Harlan shot to his feet, clapping his hands once as he did so. Fetching his walking stick that was leaning against a dusty, brown station wagon, he began to march into the dense, green undergrowth before us.

Beyond the wall of vegetation, we found ourselves surrounded by broad pine trees that soared above, a thick mist clinging to their branches so that you couldn't quite see their tops. To our left was the mighty river, easily twenty feet across at its narrowest point, with a drop of at least ten feet on the bank we stood on. Harlan pointed at the rocky, precipitous rock face.

"We'll want to stay a few feet away from the edge. This trail will lead us down a few miles before we get to a point where we can cross the river, which we will do toward the end of the day. Hope everyone packed some comfortable boots!" he snickered. I watched the short man glance down at his feet scornfully.

We followed Harlan along the narrow trail that followed the cliff edge, the pathway covered in damp, orange-brown pine needles that stuck to everything. Chuck and his brother walked behind the doctor in the line, followed by the lanky man and the woman, then myself and Harvey, where the small man had now fallen to the rear.

In the gentle morning light, I found myself entranced by our surroundings. The rich greenery that lined the path and climbed the great trunks of these trees rustled with the light breeze that carried with it the smell of the vibrant forest and crystal clear river below. Gazing out over the water and the treetops beyond the embankment on the other side, I could see a distant, solitary rock formation that seemed to jut out from its surroundings.

It towered far above the hills that lie beneath the pines, almost making it appear as though it had been added there as some afterthought, that it didn't truly belong in such an otherwise picturesque landscape. Its surface was dark and ragged, with sheer faces that ran to almost a point at its top. Very little vegetation dared to scale its sides as though there was some form of deterrence we could not yet see. It was deeply unsettling to look at and left me with a sort of discomfort wedging itself into the back of my mind.

---

After some time, we took our first break under the shade of a rocky overhang nestled in the snaking roots of a gnarled and wind-battered pine. Harlan sat with the Washburn brothers, snacking on some granola. Harvey and I joined the other group of three a few feet away. They all appeared to know each other already and were deep in conversation when we sat down.

"Arnie, those boots of yours look pretty dang new. Can't imagine you're having a great time breaking them in so far," the lanky man directed at the short one. Arnie shook his head, his husky hands massaging his feet.

"Already have some blisters forming on my soles and the big toe on my left. I knew I should've brought my old pair instead. These'll wear down all of the skin on my feet before we even make camp for the night," he chuckled in response. The spindly man raised his metal bottle as if to toast before bringing it back down for another drink. He glanced over at Harvey and me with intrigue.

"Welcome back, Harv. Heard about the wife. Congratulations! You two will make excellent parents," he said, smiling, before fixing his gaze upon me intently.

"Not sure I know your name. I'm Marcus, that's my cousin Arnold, but everyone calls him Arnie, and she's a coworker from his firm back in Pinewood, Heather," he said, gesturing to each of the other members of the group.

"I'm Sam," I added awkwardly. Marcus lifted his bottle again.

"Well, welcome aboard, Sam! Any friend of Harv is a friend of ours. You from around these parts?" he inquired. Before I could respond, Harvey jumped in enthusiastically.

"He's a pretty frequent patron at the diner. I think you all just missed him Thursday morning. We've been doing some renovations up at his place for the past week and a half. Great guy all around!"

Heather was the next to poll.

"What do you do for work, Sam?" she asked. I hesitated for a moment, searching for an appropriate response.

"I'm actually unemployed for the moment. I've been living off of my savings and a life insurance payout while I get back on my feet." Heather glanced over at the other two men to her left, exchanging looks with them.

"I'm sorry to hear about your loss. We won't ask about your past if that's something you'd rather keep to yourself," Arnie spoke, his mouth full of what was likely peanuts. He swallowed another handful, smiling at me. I expressed my gratitude to them before changing the subject, breaking some of the awkward tension that had developed.

"Anyone do this hike before?" I asked the group. Everyone but Heather shook their head.

"I did something similar back in eighty-nine, but I attempted to climb the Crag," she said, gesturing to the lonesome peak to our backs. She then rolled up her sleeve, revealing a massive scar that wrapped around her forearm and splintered into several smaller pathways.

"Got this as a souvenir for my trouble. Took me and my partner seventy hours to work our way back down the mountain and across the river, and was barely conscious for the bulk of that. Not sure how we survived that trek," she shared grimly. Harvey shuddered.

We spent the next few minutes silently eating a mid-morning meal and rehydrating in the peaceful shade of the overhang, listening to the birdsong of the forest. I found it bewildering that I had lived so close to a place like this for two years and never once ventured beyond the bar in Wendell. I knew that I would have to come back on my own after this trip. Once everyone had satisfied their appetite, Harlan stood up and motioned for us to do the same, leading us away from our place of respite.

Over the course of the remainder of the morning, we worked our way down the winding path, occasionally drifting back into the thick of the forest when detouring around larger obstacles. In these places, the mist drew in around us like an impermeable barrier, often resulting in only a few feet of visibility. During these stretches, the group would bunch up to avoid losing sight of the person in front of them.

By mid-afternoon, Harlan had brought us to a stop at the bank of the river. The drop here was much smaller at perhaps only four feet, but there was no lower ledge to keep you from plunging directly into the water. He turned to face us, a long rope bridge spanning the divide behind him.

"Alright, everyone. This is where we make our crossing. Now, the bridge is safe, but we can only do one at a time. I will go last. Do I have any volunteers who want to give it a go?"

Almost immediately, the younger Washburn brother stepped forward, arrogantly marching up to the edge of the crossing. He tested the tension of the rope with one foot before leaning onto it with the rest of his weight. It gave slightly but did not deter him as he pressed onward, quickly reaching the other side, about twenty five feet away, in a matter of moments.

The older Washburn made the journey next, though with much more consideration for what he was doing, carefully placing his feet so that they would not slip from the central chord. Once he had crossed, Arnie traversed the bridge, followed by Marcus and then Heather. Harvey looked at me next, but seeing the hesitation in my eyes, he smiled and walked over to the anchoring poles.

As he crossed the bridge, the rope seemed to give more than it had prior, dipping in the middle so that the chord nearly touched the rushing water below. However, Harvey did not seem to notice this, as he cheerfully waved when he reached the other side. I exchanged a look of concern with Harlan, who also seemed to have witnessed what I had.

"We'll take another bridge further downstream on the way back," he said. I reluctantly approached the crossing. I was not afraid of falling or the water, but something about this had me on edge. I took a deep breath and started over, using both hands to stabilize myself on the ropes to either side of my body while carefully balancing my feet on the slippery chord below. It felt sturdy enough, and the concern had subsided by the time I reached the other side. When the group reassembled, we carried on, this time into the deep of the forest, leaving the comfort of the trail behind.

---

AFTER A FEW HOURS of blazing our own way through the dense underbrush and winding down rocky hillsides, Harlan brought us to a halt in a small clearing alongside a pond. The dimming, overcast sky above was obscured by the crowded branches of the trees surrounding us. The doctor surveyed the space, examining the water feature before suddenly clapping his hands, startling all of us.

"This is where we will make camp for the night. We are lucky the water isn't stagnant, or else we'd be swarmed by mosquitos tonight," he said excitedly. Exhausted, the group unpacked their gear while Harlan assembled a fire pit from loose stones and dead tree branches.

By the time the tents were erected, the sun was setting, drawing in the dark around us as we clung to the light of the fire like moths to a flame. The world was eerily silent around us, almost as though it simply did not exist beyond the bounds of the flickering light. The shadows of the trees danced wildly as the fire burned, snapping and popping as the dry wood spat hot sap into the pit.

After settling my nerves, I joined the group as they gathered around the blaze, cooking s'mores and exchanging in light, friendly banter. I simply sat and took it all in, feeling a rush of happiness that I had not felt in years and forgetting how isolated we all were. Harvey handed me some sort of dried jerky, which I graciously accepted as I was famished.

"Anyone a fan of ghost stories?" Chuck asked the group, having finished his dinner. Harlan smiled.

"Excellent idea, Chuck!"

The older Washburn cleared his throat, theatrically spitting at the ground to his side with great enthusiasm.

"This is based on a true story. Many, many years ago, there was a doomed caravan of settlers from the East making their way through these very woods. They had foolishly left Nebraska too late into the season and were now caught in a cold, harsh winter. They sought shelter in the caves for ten days before running out of supplies. Soon, they began to get hungry and ate their animals," he paused dramatically, looking around the circle.

"But the storm continued to get worse. A few attempted to make a break for it, realizing that they were going to starve if they stayed. None of them returned. The remaining survivors grew hungry and restless. Their leader asked everyone to draw straws, the shortest of which was a boy no older than eleven. The leader wanted to retry, but they would not listen. That night, they killed him and cooked his body for food. Every day, they would draw straws and eat the one who lost until it was only the first boy's mom and the leader left. Nobody knows what truly happened next, but it is said that you can still see their spirits in these woods," he finished, seemingly pleased with his story.

"If no one survived, where the hell did you get the story from," asked Marcus. Chuck sat in silence for a moment as though he had been struck across the face, and the realization hadn't quite sunk in yet.

"Maybe someone found the cave and a journal or something," he offered. Marcus shrugged, drinking from his bottle again.

"Could be. Still a pretty generic story that could've come from anywhere."

"I've got one," piped up Heather. She readjusted herself on the ground and sat up.

"This is *actually* based on a true story," she shot a glance at Chuck, attempting to suppress the grin on her face. Chuck rolled his eyes sarcastically.

"When my partner and I first attempted to summit the Crag a few years ago, we made camp about halfway up the back slope. It was the first time either of us had tried this, and we were both excited to finish the hike in the morning, but something happened that night that I will never forget." She rolled up her shirt sleeve again to show the scar tissue to everyone.

"I was awoken by something shuffling outside of my tent. I went to investigate only to find someone standing near the ledge about five feet from our camp, facing out over the precipice. I called out to them, thinking it might be my friend, but he was still fast asleep in his tent. Curious, I got up and approached this apparition. It had wispy, black hair and a skeletal figure wearing a nightgown. But before I could get any closer, it vanished, which startled me so much that I tripped and nearly fell off the side of the mountain, tearing open my arm. To this day, I still don't know what I saw. Thankfully, my partner had heard me slip and was able to rescue me."

The group sat still, wide-eyed, picturing her story. I felt incredibly unsettled, my mind drifting back to the creature I had encountered in my dreams the week before. Her description of it was eerily similar. With that, she stood up, thanked everyone for listening, and made her way to her tent, quietly giggling as she went.

"Sweet dreams, everyone!" she called out before

crawling into her sleeping back and zipping herself into her shelter. We all sat in silence for a while longer before Harlan began to regale us with stories about his travels across the country, attempting to lighten the mood. This continued for another hour or so until the fire began to wane. We turned in for the night as Harlan doused the flames and plunged us into total, suffocating darkness.

# FIVE

Many hours had passed as I tossed and turned, unsure of if I had managed to fall asleep, echoes of Heather's story ringing out in my mind. Prior to this, I had not put much stock into what I had witnessed in my dream after consulting with Harlan, but perhaps this was all just a mere coincidence. But I could not convince myself nor deny what I had seen.

Almost as though on cue, I heard the snap of a twig just beyond the thin, orange fabric membrane of the tent I was sheltered within, the sound thundering through the silence I had previously found myself in. I felt my heart skip a beat as I lay there, anxiously waiting for another indication that something was out there. After a few moments of stillness, I reassured myself that I hadn't heard anything and that my exhausted mind was just playing tricks on me.

But then I heard another, though much further away. This time, I rearranged myself within the tight confines of my tent, inching myself up to the zipper and slowly undoing it. Peering out into the dark, I quickly realized that I couldn't see anything. Clouds had obstructed the stars and moon to the point that only a faint shimmer of light illuminated the clearing, most of it reflecting off of the ominously still pond at the base of camp. Against my better judgment, I slowly climbed out of the tent, feeling myself drawn out by some greater power beyond my comprehension.

When I was fully standing in the dark, I began surveying what I could of my surroundings. It took a few moments for my eyes to adjust enough to begin making out silhouettes. I quickly learned that the others had gone, the area around the clearing completely devoid of the tents set up alongside mine only hours prior. Feeling exposed and fighting the fear welling up in my chest, I hurried back to my shelter only to realize that it, too, was gone.

Beginning to panic, I fumbled through my pockets, procuring a small lighter from its contents. Hands trembling, I struck the flint wheel, sending sparks flying and igniting the wick. The warm light dimly illuminated my surroundings, repelling the darkness as the shadows hungrily lapped at the perimeter.

I fought the urge to cry out for help, knowing that there would be no one to hear. My next course of action was to attempt to reignite the fire pit Harlan had prepared and wait out the night to then try and find my way back at dawn, but it was no longer here. It was almost as if the camp had never existed. The gravity of the situation in which I found myself began to sink in, the fear returning. Making a crude torch from a tree branch and pine resin, I set off into the forest beyond the clearing, attempting to retrace my steps from during the day.

I felt as though I were floating through the murky black as I weaved my way through the tree trunks and underbrush, stumbling over gnarled roots and jutting rocks. I dared not look behind me as though I felt I was being pursued. I had no reason to believe that I wasn't completely alone, but I could not shake the feeling. I could sense the presence of something out in the dark, watching me.

I was unsure how long I had been moving or where I was headed, but I was surprised when I found myself at the edge of the river. I quickly looked both ways, scanning for the crossing. Seeing its outline a few hundred feet to my left, I began to rush in its direction. When I was no more than a handful of yards away, I heard what sounded like a large animal come crashing from the brush where I had exited only a moment prior.

Hearing its weight pounding on the dirt and stone behind me, I dropped my torch and sprinted for the rope bridge. It felt as though it were right behind me, ice-cold wind howling as it bore down on the back of my neck. Crashing into the first pole that anchored the bridge to this side of the river, I threw myself into the rope, scrambling to cross. I could feel my heart pounding in my throat as I thrashed, pulling my body frantically along the chord, the bridge flailing in the dark. After an agonizing minute, I had reached the other side.

Preparing to tear the anchors out of the ground so that whatever had been chasing me would be trapped, I looked back across to see what it was. But there was nothing there. My torch lay in the dirt beyond the river, its fading light illuminating the shore. Deciding not to trust the false sense of security I began to feel, I rocked the two anchoring poles until they were loose, dropping the bridge into the river.

I watched as the tangle of rope was washed downstream a ways before being submerged in the thrashing waters. Making another torch, I decided to press onward, not wanting to give my pursuer a chance to find another crossing and catch up with me. Just as the former fire I had ditched on the other side ceased burning, I heard something akin to a wild animal cry out into the night. My fears had been realized.

I ran up the path alongside the river, keeping clear from the deeper parts of the forest. I would rather scale obstructions than find myself surrounded and lost. It let out another wail, this time seemingly from my side of the waterway. It had found a way across. Reaching the same rocky protrusion we had used for shelter during our break the day before, I ducked under, frantically searching for a place to hide.

Finding such a location, I wedged myself into the crevice behind some of the roots and brush, but not before tossing the torch over the edge of the cliff and into the river. I held my breath for what felt like years, waiting for whatever was following me to catch up. And, sure enough, a shadowy figure launched itself through the area beneath the overhang at the speed of lightning, missing my hiding place by mere inches.

A few yards away, it hesitated. I peered through my cover at it, attempting to make out its features, but it was far too dark. The faint silhouette it made was hauntingly gangly, hunched over on all fours. I was unsure why it had stopped, but I could feel the panic setting in. Maybe it could smell me somehow, and knew I had stopped.

After several tormenting minutes, it continued down the path, rounding a corner, and disappeared from view. I latched my eyes shut and buried my face in my hands, whimpering silently. *I just want this to stop*, I agonized. Almost as if a wish had been granted, I felt the warmth of sunshine on my face and the muffled sound of birdsong.

Opening my eyes slowly, I found myself curled up within my tent, the fabric above me plastered with the shadows of dancing tree branches in a warm morning light. *Had I been dreaming again?* I thought to myself, still holding my breath as I listened intently to the outside. Slowly but surely, I could hear the sound of hushed laughter from the other party members, evidently trying to keep from waking anyone still sleeping up.

I unzipped the entrance to my tent, the rush of fresh air filling the space as I did so. Poking my head out, I glanced around the clearing, partially expecting to find myself trapped in the dark once more. To my relief, everything was as it had been when I went to sleep the night before, and a group of people with their backs to me, overlooking the pond.

"Welcome back to the land of the living," Harvey's voice boomed to my right, startling me. He was sitting just outside his shelter, a steaming thermos nestled between his large hands. He took another sip before holding it out to me.

"Freshly brewed coffee. Can't say it will be as good as the diner, though. Had to use pond water. But I did boil it beforehand, so you shouldn't die at least," he laughed. I exited the tent the remainder of the way, put my boots on while not bothering to lace them quite yet, and took the thermos from his hand.

"Sleep alright?" he questioned, a twinge of concern in his voice. I could only imagine what I looked like right now, but that all but confirmed it was probably not great.

"I'm not convinced I actually slept last night," I responded, taking a large gulp of the coffee. It was incredibly bitter but packed the punch I desperately needed.

"Sure looks like it. These aren't exactly the most comfortable things to sleep in, but you get used to it surprisingly quickly, especially after hiking all day," Harvey stated, the general, optimistic demeanor returning to his voice. I glanced down at my watch to check the time: 7 AM.

"Any idea what time we head out today?" I asked, to which Harvey shrugged nonchalantly.

"Beats me. The doc was up before any of us. He woke up Chuck to let him know he was checking out a potential path ahead and would be back. That was probably about an hour or so ago, so I'd imagine he'll be getting back here soon. Why?"

I hesitated, not realizing that I had just cornered myself in this conversation. Deciding that I did not want to share the details of my dream with Harvey, I opted to be more vague to avert greater concern.

"I'm just not sure about continuing on this trip. Maybe I was just expecting something different. That maybe I'd have some sort of awakening that would change my whole outlook on life and make me better, however naive that might be to think. Just not feeling right, is all. I'm thinking about heading back," I responded. Harvey stared at me for a moment, and I could tell he did not buy anything I just said but chose not to press me any further.

"That is unfortunate to hear, but it's also only been one day. You haven't given Mother Nature the chance to do anything yet. When was the last time you gave anything a shot like this?" he grilled, some of the charm and warmth in his voice fading away. I could tell I had upset him, whether by my admission of failure or that he knew I didn't tell him everything, but I knew he was right, even if it made me uncomfortable. After all, they were only dreams and couldn't hurt me.

I conceded much to the delight of Harvey, who then regaled me in his stories from his previous hikes and how he had met his wife, Cynthia, during one of those escapades. It was warming to hear the happiness in his voice and helped ease my mind off the events that had transpired. Shortly thereafter, Harlan came through the bush line just across the pond, his arms outstretched overhead like he was celebrating.

"Let's start tearing down. We're burning daylight!" he exclaimed. And just like that, everyone was up and busy at work breaking everything down, packing their supplies back into their packs. Within fifteen minutes, it was as if we were never even there, even returning the stones that made up the fire pit back to the woods. We lined up while Harlan took a quick count of everyone before setting off once more.

The hike today seemed to be up a gradual incline alongside the stream that fed into the pond. The waterway was nestled between two unassuming slopes to either side of us that proved to be somewhat challenging to navigate on account of there being very little flat space alongside the stream. The work was slow, but nobody seemed to be in much of a rush.

We had all fallen into a similar order as we had the day before, although Arnie was able to keep up with Heather and Marcus much easier, leaving Harvey and me at the rear. Nobody really talked during this stretch, which was probably for the best as the wet, mossy stones could easily lead to a broken ankle if one misjudged their step.

Eventually, the slopes leveled off, and the stream disappeared somewhere underground. We stood at the top of the glen as Harlan surveyed our surroundings and compared them against his map. From here, we changed course, hiking along the ridge line to our right. With the intermission in difficult climbing, the other members of the group began talking amongst themselves again.

"How are you holding up there, Arnie?" Harvey called out. The short man turned around, walking backward for a moment.

"Better than you, it seems. You're pretty slow today," he teased.

"Sam's the one slowing me down, so you better thank him," Harvey bellowed, elbowing me with nearly enough force to knock me over.

"Hey!" I protested, smiling. I attempted to return the favor, but I don't think there was anything I could do to move that behemoth of a man as I merely bounced off of him. The banter continued for some time, eventually pulling in Marcus and Heather, but I stayed out of it, choosing instead just to take it all in from the sideline.

We stopped for lunch not too long after at the base of a large pine tree, its lush branches sprawled out overhead. Segmenting into our groups once more, Harvey and I joined Arnie, Marcus, and Heather on the right side, nestled into a compact area between the trunk of the tree and some bramble bushes, which offered an additional level of seclusion, Marcus immediately took advantage of by relieving himself just out of view.

Once we had all settled, each member of the group retrieved something to eat from their packs. I munched away at a few dry granola bars that seemed to absorb all of the saliva in my mouth and clung to my tongue as I tried to swallow. It was very unpleasant, and I began to wonder if Harvey had packed these for me because he didn't want them himself. I listened intently to the conversations the others had started, trying to distract myself from the offensive experience in my mouth.

"And I am telling you, just because you work together doesn't mean you should be seeing each other. That's HR's worst nightmare right there," Marcus said to Arnie, who threw his hands into the air in protest.

"Come on, Marc. We've been going steady for three months now. Things are going good! Besides, we've looked at company policy, and there was nothing outlined there," he insisted.

"I've told you not to call me 'Marc', Arnold. But that still doesn't change the fact that this is just a disaster waiting to happen," Marcus teased. Arnie opened his mouth, the thought practically falling off his tongue, but he relented and remained quiet for a moment, evidently rethinking his approach.

"How are you and Jessica doing?" Heather asked Marcus, playfully nudging him with her arm. He smiled, losing himself in his thoughts for a moment. At that, I felt a twinge of sorrow, albeit fleeting. I remembered how excited I was to share news about Maria with anyone who would listen.

"She's doing great! Just started her role at that new company that came into town. 'Travel Pinewood' or something like that."

Heather looked perplexed for a moment, which urged Marcus to continue.

"I think it's some sort of regional travel marketing thing. They just opened up shop down on Main two-ish months ago. Right across from Joe's? All I know is that they got grant money for it and are part of the plan to revitalize the regional economy by boosting tourism," he elaborated. We all nodded, though I am sure most of us were just as clueless as before, judging by the lack of follow-up.

"I'm happy to hear that things are going well. I think the sooner we can move away from lumber and paper production, the better. Every time I leave Pinewood for longer than a few days, that wretched stink is all I smell when I get home," Heather said with potent disdain in her voice.

"Not everyone here wants that," came a cynical response from around the tree. Seconds later, Chuck Washburn appeared, leaning himself against the mossy trunk.

"Chuck, we all love you and your involvement in the community, but I think I speak for everyone here when I say that the only reason you stand behind those companies is because they heavily sponsor your station," Heather expressed while Chuck smirked.

"It definitely helps, but they are also critical to the local economy. 'Northwest Lumber' and 'Pine Valley Paper Products' employ probably over nine hundred people combined. Killing them off would send the region into a recession, and nobody wants to visit somewhere with no money," he responded snidely. Heather opened her mouth to protest, but Chuck cut her off before she could say anything.

"I mean no offense. I just think you need to see the big picture is all before saying such things," he concluded before disappearing behind the tree once more. Heather shook her head in disagreement.

"He does have a point, Heather," Arnie suggested timidly.

"It's not worth it," she retorted in a quiet voice, seemingly to herself.

"Who knew *both* of the Washburn brothers were kind of pricks?" I whispered to Harvey, who nodded in agreement. The tension dissipated when Harlan, who was as eager as ever, called for everyone to reassemble. We quickly finished what we were eating and congregated before him. The doctor unfolded his map and squatted down, placing the parchment on the orange pine needles that blanketed the ground.

"We've got a few more hours of hiking before we get to the spot I've outlined for us to rest for the night. Fortunately, it should be mostly level or downhill from here, so it should be easy. Everyone ready to go?"

---

As he had said, it was several more hours before we made another stop. The trek took us alongside winding hillsides and across streams nestled at their valley floors, the waters nearly crystal clear as they trickled down their rocky riverbeds. I enjoyed these parts of the hike the most, I think. The air was always filled with the chatter of birds and the drone of insects. Everything felt so alive yet so simple; it was vindicating in a way to know that despite everything that had gone so wrong, things would just continue on, undaunted.

Eventually, we came to a halt in a meadow that rested on a wind-battered hillside, a crisp breeze sweeping across the wildflowers and long grasses, undulating like waves on an ocean. The view overlooked a basin where a deep and impenetrable lake with the most vivid, mesmerizing blue water pooled. The shape of the feature vaguely resembled that of an elongated rectangle, though the sides bowed inward and its length stretched for at least a mile. It left me wishing I remembered to pack my camera.

We spread ourselves out in the vast space left by the clearing. I watched as Arnie began picking a few of the wildflowers to gift to Marcus and Heather, who both accepted with grandiose gestures. Harvey had disappeared behind a small cluster of knotted trees, likely to take care of unfinished business from the last stop. Jakob and his brother, Chuck, simply stood there, taking everything in.

But before I could do anything, Harlan had snuck up behind me.

"I've been meaning to check in with you. I was pleasantly surprised to receive your call last week saying that you'd like to join in on the expedition. Now that you've got nearly two days under your belt, how are you feeling? This is completely off the books, by the way," he asked sincerely.

"I had my doubts, and I suppose I still have them, but this has gone a lot better than I was expecting. I do feel a sense of peace being out here. But I had this really strange nightmare last night. It felt a lot like the one I told you about the last time I was at your office," I replied. He looked at me, concern flickering in his eyes for one brief second.

"Anything I should know about?" he queried. There was something about his voice that I couldn't quite put my finger on.

"Not really. I think Heather's story got me a little worked up, and being out in the wilderness probably just amplified it."

He stood there for a moment in silence. He reached out and squeezed my arm with more force than I expected.

"Come find me if it happens again," was all he said before trodding down the hill, his head tilted upward as he examined the sky and the darkening clouds overhead. Shortly after, he called everyone to him, a sense of urgency in his tone. We collected tightly around him as the wind picked up.

"Chuck, in your professional, meteorological opinion, those look like rain clouds, don't they?" he asked, motioning to the clouds. Chuck examined them for a few seconds, likely also pausing for dramatic effect, before confirming the doctor's suspicions.

"Rain. Looks like it might be heavy. And judging by the

height and structure of that cloud there: thunderstorm," he said, pointing to a lone cloud near the front, whose shape resembled that of an anvil. Harlan looked at his map again, hastily running his finger over it in seemingly random lines before coming to a stop.

"Since I don't think we are going to want to be exposed to this tonight, we're going to follow this ridge for maybe another mile. This'll put us off course for the day, but there is a ranger cabin on the next hill over that should keep us out of the storm."

With that, we were off once more, a newfound gravity in our steps as the clouds loomed in. Gone were the pleasant sounds of wildlife, replaced instead by the howl of wind as the gusts whipped through the treetops and down the valleys. It was as though the world itself had turned against us as we scrambled for shelter. Glancing over my shoulder, I could see the dark, glimmering curtain of rain bearing down near the far side of the lake, the wall of precipitation appearing opaque.

The lake was now a murky grey capped with foamy, white waves that rocked its surface as the wind blew it in our direction. The memory I had of first seeing it was now tainted by the ominous facsimile before me. Then came a flash and the low grumble of distant thunder. Harlan called out, "It's right there!" gesturing at a squat, log cabin with a moss-covered roof positioned just inside the tree line a few hundred feet ahead. Just as the drizzle started upon us, we were barreling through the heavy door.

The inside was dark and musty, feeling as though we were the first here in a very long time. The area we directly found ourselves crowding contained a simple dining table lined with worn stools with warped legs, a dinette with a wood-burning stove, a metallic washbasin, and doorless cabinets in which sat an assortment of pans and plates. To our immediate right was a fireplace comprised of fieldstone and a deep hearth, surrounded by a few chairs.

Harlan reached into a pocket and handed me a small aluminum flashlight, beckoning me to turn it on while he refolded his crumpled map. Illuminating the space for the group, I noted a few doorways near the back of the structure, likely leading to sleeping quarters. There was also a mountain of chopped firewood stacked to the far right of the main room, partially obscuring one of the few windows in the structure.

By now, the wind had picked up and pounded the walls, howling all around us. The torrents of rain beat against the glass panes in an undulating pattern, completely enshrouding the outside world. It was strange to feel this helpless to a storm I would have otherwise thought of as nothing more than an inconvenience had I been traveling into town or completing some other mundane task. I felt as though I were trapped aboard a sinking ship on the open ocean.

Distracting myself from the intruding thoughts, I hurried over to the firewood, piling up a few pieces under my arms to deliver to the hearth. Dropping to my knees, I unwound the twine that bound the wood together and began stacking them into a pyramid. Realizing that I was still missing some components, I got up and searched through the open cabinets for anything I could use as tinder.

Finding some incredibly old and musty newspapers, I returned to the fireplace, packing the parchment into balls and tucking them into the base of my structure. Satisfied with my work, I withdrew my lighter from my pocket, striking the flint wheel to spawn a flickering yellow flame. Shielding it with my cupped hand, I lowered it down to the tinder, igniting the paper. Within seconds, the growing flames hungrily climbed the firewood, swallowing it whole.

I sat back on my haunches, basking in the warm, orange glow before me. It reminded me of going camping with my father growing up and how he taught me the process of building a fire. I'm sure he would have been proud to see this one. Deciding not to dwell on old memories, I stood up, brushing the grime off of my knees and palms.

"Hey, great fire, Sam!" Harvey bellowed, slamming his large hand on my upper back with nearly enough force to send me flailing into the flames. Reacting quickly, he clenched my jacket to stabilize me.

"Sorry about that," he said quietly.

"It's fine. You're just too strong for your own good. But a heads up in the future would be appreciated," I responded, letting out a slight chuckle. Turning around, I noticed that nearly everyone, excluding the doctor, had gathered around in the seating area behind us, evidently also seeking the warmth of my fire.

"How'd you learn to make one like that so quickly?" Arnie queried, pointing at the pyramid I had built, blazing away.

"It was what my father taught me when we went camping. There's nothing special about it. Just have to give the flames room to breathe. I'm sure if he was here, he'd probably tell me I did something wrong with it..." I trailed off, getting lost in my memories. *I don't remember the last time I spoke to him. I don't even know if he's still alive,* I thought, a flood of regret washing over me for a moment.

"Wow. What a riveting story. Now, can you move out of the way? You're blocking the heat," Jakob groaned, lounging awkwardly on a bench so that nobody else could share it, the irritation in his tone palpable. I glared directly at him.

He had all the mannerisms of a spoiled child in the way he presented himself and the way he spoke. Sensing the tension simmering in the room, Chuck, who was standing to the side, muttered something unintelligible to his brother before addressing me.

"Disregard him. Ma never told him 'no,' and his frontal lobe isn't fully functioning yet. He's an embarrassment to me and the family."

There was some muffled snickering amongst the other members of the group. Immediately, Jakob sat up, puffing out his chest like some sort of bird facing down a much larger, intimidating foe, scowling at everybody.

"Settle down, won't you? This isn't like back home. Ma sent you up here because she was sick and tired of your shit, and you aren't exactly doing yourself any favors. I'm sure she'd love to hear how you're picking fights with strangers again," Chuck grumbled. Their relationship sounded more akin to a child and parent rather than siblings, leaving me feeling somewhat bad for the older Washburn, who likely hadn't intended for his arrogant brother to join this trip.

As the space warmed up, the group dispersed, each clique finding a spot to eat a warm meal and discuss the adventures from the day. I occasionally listened in whenever Harvey's booming voice overpowered the others, the topic of conversation often drifting to his days sailing the Great Lakes or his antics at the diner back in Ackerman. However, I decided I would sit down by the hearth alone, watching the shroud of night descend on us through the window.

# SIX

The storm progressed throughout the night, making it difficult to get any proper rest. This was further compounded by the fact that I still had no answers for the experiences I had dreamt of the night before, leaving me feeling uneasy about the prospect of falling asleep. Conceding defeat sometime in the middle of the night, I rolled out of the bottom bunk I had seized only a few hours prior. It groaned as I righted myself, the lumpy and disheveled bed leaving an indentation where I had lain.

A flash of lightning briefly illuminated the dark, shadowy bunk room through the single window to my right. The walls were composed of long, pine logs that stretched the lengths of the shelter, the spaces between filled with some sort of dark, insulating agent. There were clusters of crudely erected bunks with enough room to sleep twelve people, though I highly doubted anyone unfortunate enough to rest here would get any amount of sleep due to how horrendously uncomfortable the beds were.

Directly before me was the doorway that led back out into the main room, the faintest orange glow lining the edges of the closed door, signifying that my fire was still smoldering beyond. Lowering my legs the rest of the way to the floor, I cautiously shuffled toward my exit, careful not to upset the floorboards and awaken the others, who had all somehow managed to fall into a deep sleep. There was another bolt of lightning and a deep, growling thunder shortly afterward that I used to mask the creek of the door as I slipped into the main space.

I stumbled over to a chair to the left of the fireplace, the flickering flames causing the elongated shadows of the furniture legs to dance wildly and made it difficult to gauge where exactly I was stepping. It wasn't until I sat down that I realized Harlan was huddled in the chair directly across from me, tucked away in the corner of the room, partially obscured by the fieldstone that jutted from the mantle of the fireplace. It was difficult to tell if he was awake or not for a moment, but he shifted when a globule of pine resin leaked from the burning wood and dropped into the fire below it, popping loudly. He glanced up at me through his glasses, the majority of his facial features cast in sinister shadows that fluttered with the crackle of the flames.

"Hey doc..." I started, uneasy and unsure how to strike up a conversation in this awkward situation. He adjusted his seat, dragging the legs along the floorboards so that his figure was more visible in the dim light. Yet his face remained cast in an impermeable shadow.

"Having trouble sleeping, are we, Samuel?" Harlan asked, hushed. There was a loud crack of thunder that shook the cabin and rattled the glass panes of the windows. Something felt wrong here, but I convinced myself that my nerves were getting to me, likely a combination of the tension and lack of sleep. What I really needed was to talk to someone.

"Yes, doc. I cannot get my mind off of my dreams, especially the one I was telling you about last night," I muttered in response.

"Do you want to talk about it some more?"

"Yes, if that is okay."

Harlan, crossing his arms across his chest, leaned back in his chair, the wood joints squeaking under the shifting weight. He gestured for me to proceed. "What seems to be the trouble?"

I breathed in deeply, searching for a place to start.

"As I said, this might just be related to Heather's story from the other day, but the way she described that thing, it just feels like it is related to what I saw in my hallway in the dream I was telling you about during our last session. And then, I had this other dream that I was all alone in the wilderness. I had to try and find my way back out of the forest, but I felt like I was being watched and followed the whole time."

"Did you see anything coming after you?" the doctor asked. I shook my head, closing my eyes so I could be in the dark of the forest once more.

"What can you tell me about your surroundings? What did you hear?"

I found his last question somewhat odd, so I asked for clarification.

"What do you mean by 'what did you hear'? I didn't hear anything."

The doctor leaned forward, resting his elbows on his knees, the shadows dancing across his face and the glow of the fire glinting on his dirty spectacles.

"Interesting. Did you know that there is a natural occurrence wherein all living animals, or creatures, become silent in the presence of a predator? It is fascinating when you think about it," he said in an unsettling whisper, his words almost lost in the sound of the torrents of rain clattering on the roof overhead.

"What's that got to do with the rest of the dream?" I asked hesitantly. Despite his face still being obscured, I could see his mouth curl into an unsettling, toothy smile.

"You were being hunted, Samuel."

By now, I was thoroughly distressed, having realized that engaging in this conversation seemed to have the exact opposite effect I had been hoping for. I let out a forced chuckle, glancing around the room nervously, waiting for him to admit this was some kind of sick, twisted joke.

"Well, I can't say this has helped much, but I think I'm going to give those bunk beds another shot. Thank you for listening, doctor," I said in an attempt to excuse myself, slowly standing back up.

"I don't think we're done yet, son."

I stopped in my tracks. The doctor's voice had changed, replaced instead with a deeper, gravelly one. I looked back over in his direction. In the place formerly occupied by Harlan sat a much older man with crew cut, greying hair, tired blue eyes, and a thick beard. Against all sense, it was my father.

"Dad?" I asked in disbelief. The man nodded, a brief smile crossing his lips. He beckoned for me to sit back down as he inspected the fire.

"I taught you well, son. You've gone and made your old man proud."

I was furiously rubbing my eyes, convinced that I was just seeing things in my sleep-deprived state. Yet he was still there, smiling at me.

"Dad... I meant to call... I'm sorry. I'm so, so sorry," I

stammered, searching for words that failed to materialize as my eyes welled up.

"I know, son. Your mother and I cannot begin to understand the pain you went through... that you are still going through. All we wanted was to be there for you if you needed us," my father said in his gruff but sincere voice. I could feel myself melting in such a way that I hadn't felt in years, collapsing from my chair and onto the floor, sobbing cathartically. He got up and knelt down next to my head, resting a hand on it so that I could feel his fingers in my hair.

"I need you to do something for me. Do you think you can do that?" he asked me somberly. I looked up at him through the tears in my eyes.

"Anything..."

"I need you to forgive yourself," my father said, our gazes locking. I sat back up, wiping my eyes with the shirt sleeve.

"What for?" I questioned. His face darkened.

"For what happened to Maria. It wasn't your fault."

I shook my head, trying to put everything together and make sense of what was happening.

"But it was, Dad. It was *ALL* my fault," I responded, flustered.

"Son. This is serious. You are in grave danger. You know it," he said coldly. The energy in the conversation and room shifted abruptly.

"What do you mean?"

He pulled me up off of the floor and sat me back down in my chair, tossing a worried glance back at the fire, which had become nothing more than smoldering embers. In the dying light, I looked up at his darkening face, the features slowly disappearing into the shadows.

"You need to forgive yourself. The dead don't forgive,

Sam," the icy words hissed from my father's mouth. He looked at the remains of the fire once more.

"What does that mean, Dad? What's wrong?" I asked, feeling the dread begin to crawl its way up my chest. There was another crack of lightning, but no thunder followed as the world around me fell silent, including the sound of the rain on the wooden roof.

"Run," he whispered, the single word echoing in the void around us. Almost immediately, the light of the fire ceased as though it had been out for hours already. The air around me grew ice-cold. I scanned the room, realizing now that my father was gone. Initially, I told myself that I had slept-walked out here and just came to. How else would I have just had a conversation with my father? But I felt the sensation that I was being watched.

With another flash of lightning, I was horrified to see the same skeletal face of the creature from my dreams peeking in through the window next to the fire, its long, dark hair draped over its sunken, gray eyes. I felt my heart leap from my chest as I was plunged into pure terror. Without thinking, I bolted for the bunk room, hearing the cabin door fly open as it slammed against the wall. I flung the door shut behind me, hastily propping a chair up under the handle to keep it from opening. Searching the room, my gaze fell upon the window. It was my only way out.

The creature was now pummeling the bunk room door behind me, letting out its deep, guttural moans between the clattering of its teeth. Without checking to see if the others were there or not, I tossed open the window and dove into the rainy blackness beyond. Barreling into the thick of the woods, I heard the clash of the door failing behind me in the dark.

Weaving my way down the slopes and shielding my

eyes with my arm, I worked my way through the foliage. There was no time to make another torch, nor would it likely work here. The curtains of rain were pelting me along with the needly branches of the pine trees. In the rush of it, my foot struck a wet stone at an awkward angle, causing me to slip. Crashing to the forest floor, I rolled down the slope for a few seconds, my head bashing against other protrusions.

With no time to assess my situation and with adrenaline pumping through my veins, I immediately stood up and stumbled the rest of the way. I could hear it behind me, lumbering somewhere in the darkness. There was no time to stop.

Eventually, after what felt like hours of running aimlessly, I burst through a wall of underbrush to find myself before the same rope bridge that spanned the same river from my previous dream. *Had I really found this place again?* I thought to myself, trying to determine the likelihood I could've returned here without knowing the way. Realizing what had to be done, I hurried across the river, my feet slipping on the wet chord and the wind tossing the bridge beneath me.

Once I reached the other side, I whipped around to find the creature standing on the other shore, staring directly at me. It was hunched over on all fours, its head cocked to one side and its hollow mouth gaping as if its jaw was almost detached from the rest of its skull. As it attempted to cross the bridge, I tore out the anchoring poles to either side of me, tossing the wood and rope over the ledge and into the roaring river below. It thrashed as its gaunt body was submerged in the raging waters, becoming ensnared in the mess, before letting out an inhuman, abrasive wail and sinking into the black torrent below.

Unsure if that would be enough to stop its pursuit, I continued along the path, passing the rocky overhang I had hidden under the previous time. I did not want to test my luck there a second time. Following the winding trail along the ledge that meandered into the dark, foreboding forest, I found myself recalling less and less of the notable features I remembered during our first day of the hike.

However, just when I began to doubt my direction, I found myself standing in the muddy clearing where we had parked, only this time, it was just my truck in the desolate lot. I scrambled to the driver-side door, throwing it open as I clambered inside. I rummaged through my jacket pockets only to realize that I did not have my keys. My heart sank as I remembered leaving them with my pack at the foot of my bunk back at the cabin.

I closed the truck door, locking it behind me, and lay down. Curling up into a ball and squeezing my eyes shut, I silently begged to wake up from this agonizing nightmare. I did not know where the creature that was pursuing me was, and I knew that I was exposed here. *If it could now tear through doors, what would stop it from breaking into the cab and getting me?* And, as if by some miracle, my watch began beeping at me from under my jacket sleeve: 5 AM.

---

AND THERE I WAS AGAIN, back on the lumpy bunk mattress, nestled beneath a woolen blanket and my loose jacket, the smell of damp wood permeating the musty air in the room. I lifted my arm, the watch still chiming away, examining its face to confirm the time. Letting out a deep breath, I silenced it before dropping my head back down onto the mattress. To say I was exhausted was an understatement; instead, feeling as though I had spent the entire night racing through the forest and being pursued by the unknown entity.

Laying there, I could hear the sound of conversation beyond the closed door. Though, it was some time before I found myself ready to stir. I was more intent on listening to the muffled small talk and hushed laughter, finding it comforting to know that I was on the other side once more. As the early light of the morning sun shined through the window, growing in its strength, I climbed out of the bunk and tossed my loose jacket over my shoulder.

Placing weight down on my feet as I attempted to stand, I felt a searing pain shoot up my leg from my ankle. Looking down, I examined the joint to find that it was bruised and swollen. After a moment, I remembered that it was the same foot that I had slipped on during the dream, and somehow the injury manifested itself here.

*Or did it really happen?* I wondered. I shook my head, consoling myself. Looking back down at my ankle, the bruising had vanished, and the pain felt like an echo. Not giving myself the opportunity to dwell on it more, I threw on my worn boots and hurried through the closed door.

Beyond it, in the main room, the others were crowded around the fireplace once more, merrily talking amongst themselves while eating what appeared to be jerky and crackers. Harvey sat in the middle of the bench, flanked by Arnie and Marcus. Heather sat in the same chair I took in my dream the night prior, across from Jakob, the two seemingly in a deep debate about something I could not make out.

I continued scanning the room until my eyes fell upon Harlan and Chuck, both of whom were facing away from the rest, huddled closely together in a discussion within the cooking area. I could not make out the doctor's face, but Chuck appeared to be deeply troubled and looked as though he also did not sleep last night, his bloodshot eyes seeming to have sunken into his skull. Creeping closer to try and make out the topic of their conversation, I took a seat at the dining table.

"I'm telling you. Just like the last one, Harlan. These things are getting more and more concerning," Chuck muttered, a twinge of unease in his words. The doctor nodded, tapping his chin with an index finger, evidently deep in thought.

"I will make a note of this, and we can pick this up when we get back. Just let me know if they continue or if anything changes," Harlan responded quietly. The two quickly dispersed after that, rejoining the rest of the group as though nothing had occurred. However, I found myself wondering what they were discussing and knew that I would need answers. There was something wrong with this trip, and I might not be the only one feeling it now.

---

With the rain clearing up, we packed our things and gathered in the main room around Harlan, who was reviewing his maps. He was noticeably different today compared to his usual, cheerful self we had all come to see during the first two days of the hike. But I was fairly certain nobody else had picked up on this, perhaps instead chalking it up to a poor night's sleep. However, I exchanged a glance with Chuck, who I caught staring at me.

As we departed the cabin, I hung back with him, motioning for Harvey to join the others, as did Chuck with his younger brother. The two of us marched in silence some distance behind the rest of the group for a while, perhaps an hour or two, before either one of us spoke. I think we were both unsure of how to broach the subject we wanted to discuss. Finally, he relented with a sort of exasperation.

"I overheard your conversation with the doctor in the meadow yesterday. You mentioned having these... dreams," he started before trailing off. I shot a glance forward, making sure that the rest of the group was far enough ahead to be out of earshot. It helped that the forest itself was alive with the sounds of the morning.

"Yes. I've had them for years, but something has changed recently. They've gotten darker now. And... there's something there with me," I muttered. Chuck looked me over as though he regretted bringing it up, perhaps comparing himself to me and disliking the notion that he might have a problem that a nobody, such as myself, would also have as though it were beneath him.

Both of the Washburn brothers shared a level of arrogance and self-importance that honestly made them insufferable to interact with. It could be seen in the way they dressed and groomed or the way they both talked, like everyone was beneath them. I made a mental note to find a different radio station to tune into once this hike had concluded, as I could not, in good conscience, continue listening to him.

"What did you see?" Chuck asked hesitantly after several more minutes of walking in silence, with only the hammering sound of a woodpecker to break up the monotony. *Maybe it's not below you, after all?* I thought to myself, desperately wanting to say it aloud, but I held my tongue.

"Honestly, I am not entirely sure. The first time I saw this... thing... was in this vivid dream that I almost thought was real. It was hiding in the dark of my hallway back home, just staring at me with these sunken, dead eyes. It was gangly with grey skin. Almost looked like a skele—"

"With short, white hair, right? I think we saw the same thing!" he interrupted, seemingly pleased with himself for putting together a puzzle. I shook my head.

"Mine had long, black hair."

Chuck came to a dead stop in his tracks, glaring at me.

"But it still came after you, right?" he asked cautiously. The world around us seemed to grow quieter for a second, and I could've sworn the temperature dropped by a few degrees, but I convinced myself that it was only the shade of the trees surrounding us.

"With a voracity I have never seen in my life…"

Chuck was looking around us, perhaps also noticing the shift in the air. Grabbing him by the shoulder, I gave him a quick shake to snap him back.

"We better keep moving. They've gone out of view," I said to him, gesturing to the empty footpath ahead and the distant sound of our colleagues fading. Once we got moving again, I felt relief as the air around us warmed, carrying the gentle song of the birds high above.

"Did you have a dream last night?" Chuck asked as we rounded a bend in the way, skirting around a large, protruding mound.

"Yes. It was the worst one yet. You?"

He nodded, looking down at his boots as if ashamed.

"I was back home, on our family ranch down near Amarillo. But I was the only one there. No Ma, no Pa, and definitely not my idiot brother," he scoffed before continuing, "It was just me. All alone in the middle of the night on ten acres, miles away from civilization. I spent a few hours just walking around, even finding myself star-gazing at one point. But all the while, I felt like I was being watched.

Eventually, I ran and hid in the farmhouse back in my old bedroom. I could hear something slamming doors inside with me, going from room to room, closet to closet. When it finally got to where I was hiding, I could see it through the cracks in the door. That is exactly how you described it, minus the long hair. It turned slowly to look at me like it knew I was there, but I woke up before it got me. The damn thing had blood or something oozing from its mouth like some kind of horror movie monster."

His eyes glazed over as he finished his story, as though he was transported back to the dream and was reliving it as we spoke. Gone was the arrogance in his demeanor, instead replaced with the familiar hollowness of a broken man. Perhaps I had been too quick to judge him.

"What do you think it is?" Chuck asked, turning to me. I shrugged.

"I don't know, but I don't think it is a coincidence the two of us had a similar experience. Hell, remember Heather's story from the first night? Doesn't that also sound like it could be the same thing?"

Neither one of us spoke again for a long while, instead just walking alongside each other in silence.

---

The remainder of that day's hike took us to the base of the ridge, and up the far side of the lake we glimpsed from the meadow yesterday afternoon. The deep blue water was still as it glimmered under the waning sunlight, adding to the sense of unease I felt about it before. However, I was far more distracted by the amount of mosquitoes to contend with all the way down here as they relentlessly harassed the group in a cloud of high-pitched buzzing.

As the day grew longer, we came to our final stop at the far end of the basin. Nestled between a cluster of enormous boulders, we made our camp for the night. Unlike with the previous days, the merriment was diminished, instead replaced by a stillness, likely the result of a number of factors, including needing to make up lost ground from yesterday and all-round poor sleep in the cabin. At least, that's what I had hoped it was.

Once camp had been established, I joined Harvey down on the rocky shore of the lake, skipping palm-sized stones across the placid waters. I could tell that he was enthralled to see me after we had spent the better part of the day apart, and he regaled me with the conversations he had with the others, most of which seemed uninspired.

"So what did you and the weatherman have to talk about?" he interrogated. The suddenness of the question and deadpan delivery, accompanied by a blank expression, had me worried for a second before he let out a deep laugh.

"I'm only kidding. Whatever it was, I'm sure it was important and none of my business." He launched another stone across the water, achieving four skips before it slipped below the surface.

"It's probably best if I don't talk about it, in all honesty," I said as I plopped myself down onto the rocks below. Harvey sat down next to me, tossing his last stone to the side.

"I'm no doctor, but you can talk to me if you ever need to. Everyone needs a hand now and then, and there ain't no shame in it. Nobody was built to carry the weight of the world alone."

"You're a good man, Harvey. I wish I could be more like you."

He chuckled at that before letting out a sigh. "My wife

might disagree with you, but I am just trying my best to make the world a better place, one day at a time."

We both remained on the shore, watching the sun dip below the hills before returning to the camp to join the others for a hot meal and to share more stories under the clear night sky while I mentally prepared myself for sleep.

# SEVEN

I HAD HOPED that this night would fare better than the previous two, and, at first, I was pleasantly surprised. The first few hours were spent peacefully listening to the chirp of the crickets and the drone of other insects beyond the confines of my tent. At a few points, I had been tempted to get up and return to my spot beside the lake just to take it all in, alone, but I refrained from anything that might draw me away from the allure of slumber, or the false safety of my tent.

After finally nodding off, I found myself a passenger in a series of formulaic dreams that delivered my consciousness from one point to another, much like any ordinary night. There would also be periods where there was simply nothing, merely waiting patiently in the darkness for the next experience where time had no meaning. It wasn't until much later that things took an unfortunate shift in tone.

Sometime after waking up to relieve myself, I began to experience auditory hallucinations; someone was calling my name. At first, I had thought, and possibly hoped, that it might be one of the others from the camp attempting to play some kind of prank on me, but it was the quiet and stillness surrounding me that began to set me on edge.

Rounding the tree I had used to privacy, I found myself standing in a well-groomed yard before a stately, two-story Cape Cod, with white vinyl siding and large bay windows on the first floor. The firetruck-red front door was ajar, letting the warm evening sunlight into the entryway. With the realization of what I was seeing sinking in, I attempted to turn around, finding that no matter which way I faced, I was always looking back at the house.

I stood there for what felt like an eternity, simply refusing to budge and hoping that it might end on its own if enough time passed. But the sun never set, instead clinging to its spot low in the sky, wrapped in the brilliant colors of the sunset. It was a gorgeous night, but one I never wanted to relive. Unfortunately, I have had this particular dream almost every single night for the past two years.

Eventually, there came a loud explosion, a ball of flames erupting from the back half of the house, which caused part of the floor above to crumple and cave in. Hearing cries for help, I found myself compelled to spring into action despite knowing how this would all end. I flew through the open doorway and into a nautical-themed living area that was being swarmed by a roaring blaze. To my right was a staircase trimmed with fine wood of exquisite craftsmanship, only to be engulfed in the raging flames.

Ascending the stairs, I could hear the cries for help growing louder. Near the top was a short table with a singular vase resting upon it, and, for a moment, I snapped out of the state I was in. Unlike all of my other times experiencing this same dream, the contents of this vessel had been freshly cut lilies that I had fetched from the garden that morning. These flowers had long since wilted and dried up so that they were dark brown husks, their dead petals lying on the carpeted hallway floor.

However, the cries for help continued, and I resumed my mission in vain. Reaching the end of the hallway, I began pounding on the final door from which the shouting was emanating, the woman on the other side sobbing. But no matter what I tried, the door would not open. It was almost as though there was no room beyond it, that it might eventually give way only to reveal a solid brick wall.

By now, the flames were devouring the walls in the hallway, searing my skin as I struggled to get into the room. As my vision began to wane, I heard the click of the door latch, and it slammed open with such a massive force as though all of my efforts, across countless nights, compounded into a single moment. A great, howling wind blew from within, putting the fire out and shrouding the space in darkness. Hurrying to my feet, I backed away from the unnatural blackness of the room, taking a moment to notice that the crying had stopped.

"Maria?" I called out cautiously. There was no response. Fearing what might come next, I hurried back down the hallway and descended the stairs only to find myself back where I had started, standing before the void beyond the final door at the end of the hall. Beginning to panic, I repeated the same process several more times, each with the same exact outcome, each resulting in terror catching on in my chest and throat.

After perhaps a dozen or so attempts, I found myself back on the charred first floor. The wicked machinations, beyond my control, seemed to have finally given up. As I stepped back outside, I watched as the sun dipped below the tree tops and the final light stretched thinly across the landscape, an eerie yet all too familiar, suffocating silence drowning the world out. Then came the sound of violent thrashing from within the burnt home, and I knew it was time to run.

Spilling out onto a desolate road I did not recognize, I sprinted its length, flickering streetlights overhead that jolted to life against the darkening sky. The air surrounding me was suffocatingly cold, almost as though it were in the middle of an especially brutal winter. The creature, somewhere to my rear, let out a roar that echoed out the empty street and sent a chill down my spine. I could tell it was gaining ground on me, the sound of gnashing teeth and heavy breathing drawing closer and closer until I could've sworn I felt its ice-cold breath on the nape of my neck.

Seeing an opening in the tall shrubbery that lined the avenue, I ducked through, seemingly avoiding an attack as I heard the creature let out a frustrated cry and crash onto the asphalt. Finding myself in an overgrown, unkempt yard, I dropped into the waist-high grass and slowly backed into the shadow of a great oak. Seconds later, my pursuer barreled through the opening and along the path I did not follow, winding up a gradual incline toward a derelict home with a rotting, wooden exterior, disappearing through the open doorway and the void beyond.

Out of my view, it began violently thrashing what sounded like furniture and glassware, frustrated that I had gotten the slip on it again. But something in me would not let me get up, possibly frozen in place by the sheer terror this thing brought me. I began trying to wake myself up, repeating any of the steps I had used in the past occurrences to get out of this nightmare, but none would work. And then, the beast fell silent.

I waited, holding my breath for minutes or hours, wondering if it might reappear and find me hiding beneath this tree, but it did not. Finally convinced that I should leave, I managed to silently climb to my feet, my legs shaking beneath me as I uneasily shuffled toward the opening in the hedges. To my surprise and relief, the creature did not reemerge from the dilapidated structure, allowing me to slip back onto what I thought would be the barren road, only to find that I was standing at the edge of the lake again, the calm waters lapping at the stones I had watched Harvey skip earlier.

For a second, I thought, and hoped, that I had woken back up and had somehow managed to sleepwalk myself from the camp to the water's edge, but these were quickly dashed when I remembered just how cold and quiet everything was. Without any other thoughts and no signs of the creature, I stumbled back up the shore to our tents. Reaching my shelter, I quickly unzipped the front flap. Before I could shut myself back inside, a hand shot out of the darkness and caught my wrist, causing my heart to jump.

"Hey. Are you good?"

It was Heather, her voice groggy as though she had just woken up moments prior. I pulled my hand away, causing her to nearly fall forward. She knelt down, rubbing her eyes.

"Sorry. You gave me a start," I responded cautiously, fearing that this confrontation would be the same as the night prior with my father.

"You got up a few minutes ago, sounding like you were talking to someone, and then ran down to the lake. Watched you take a spill on those stones," she said, gesturing to the open wound I did not notice on my left knee. "Sleepwalk often, Sam?"

I shook my head. *There is no way that this is real,* I thought to myself. But by now, the cold was subsiding, and I could begin to hear the soft sounds of the forest again, though they were still muted and distant. I let out a deep breath, feeling as though I had held it this whole time.

"What were you doing up?" I asked. I noticed the hesitation as she thought about how to answer.

"Couldn't sleep. Decided to sit on one of the boulders and just watch the stars." She reached into her pocket, retrieved some bandages, and held them out to me, which I promptly took.

"About that ghost story you told the other nigh—"

"What about it?" Heather interrupted coldly. Taken aback, I shrugged and held up a hand. Seconds later, she let out a frustrated sigh. "What do you want to know?"

"Did it do anything?"

She paused, thinking her response over.

"Not that time, no."

"So you've seen it again since then?"

She nodded slowly, tossing a hurried glance over her shoulder into the dark. "Last night, I had another dream, and it was there, following me through the woods."

I could tell that she was hesitant to continue sharing.

"Chuck has seen something similar, too. Same with me. I don't know what it is, but the three of us all describe this ghostly, gaunt figure in our dreams. I don't know about your case, but it has been actively trying to attack us, but I always wake up before it gets to me..."

"Did you just see it again?" she asked, concern in her wavering voice. I nodded my confirmation, watching her eyes lose focus, adrift in deep thought.

"What do you know about it? Is it some kind of omen?" I probed, but she did not respond to my questions.

"When the sun comes back up, I think we need to

convince Harlan to take us back. There is something wrong with this place."

I stared at her, perplexed.

"But haven't you been out here before with this same group? Hell, you were the one to nearly summit the Crag and told us that story. This doesn't make any sense to me," I whispered, trying to keep my frustration from boiling over and waking up the others. There was more to this than Heather was letting on like she knew what we were up against and simply refused to elaborate.

"This group has gone on hikes in the past, yes, but this is our first outing across the river. Most of the previous ones went south. And I only did the Crag once. This is my second time coming this far up north in this wilderness," she returned. Then, from within the darkness beyond the boundaries of the camp came the snap of a twig somewhere in the underbrush, causing both of us to jump. It was still ominously quiet. Heather tossed a glance in the general direction the sound came from before whirling back around to face me, her face stoic.

"If you want to know more, we can talk when we are safely back across the river." With that, she excused herself and returned to her tent, leaving me alone with more questions than answers and a haunting feeling in the pit of my stomach. Something bad was about to happen.

---

Despite my best efforts, I was unable to calm myself down enough to get any more rest that night. Instead, the time was spent listening to the sound of the waves on the lake washing over the rocky shoreline and trying to imagine myself back in the comfort of my bed back home. But there was no respite to come, no matter how much I hoped I might open my eyes and find myself waking up there as if this was all just one bad dream.

My mind drifted back to the most recent encounter I had with this creature and the ferocity it carried. It seemed that it was becoming more aggressive with each passing time, perhaps in relation to how deep we had entered this forest. *Could they be related? Heather sounds like she is convinced of that,* I thought to myself.

Returning to my reflection, I considered the significance of the second house I found myself hiding at. It did not seem to carry any importance as I did not recognize its decaying facade and overgrown yard. However, pressing forward, I began to visually dissect the structure, imagining it in what might've been its prime many years prior before it fell into a state of such neglect. My heart sank when the realization set in: it was the home I had purchased with Maria just a few months before her passing.

After finally securing a better-paying job in the insurance industry, we pulled the trigger on settling into a two-story house on a corner lot where we might start a family. It had felt as though the entire world was falling into place at the time. She had set up an art studio in one of the small bedrooms so that it would overlook the garden she had started in the backyard that spring. I still remembered the smell of the flowers through the open kitchen windows as I made us breakfast on those crisp, early summer mornings. How I longed for those days again, my heart aching to hear her sing as she worked.

Feeling hollowed out by the agonizing trek through my memories, I got up and exited my tent, making my way back down to the lake, all the while stumbling in the dim moonlight. It reflected peacefully off of the water, which had grown still and quiet. Standing at its black edge, I found myself tempted to leap into its murkiness and let myself sink to its bottom. It pulled on me, calling my name with its mesmerizing vastness. I was not much of a believer in an afterlife, but I hoped that I was wrong—that I might see her again when all of this was over and after I atoned for what I had done.

---

After waiting several more hours, the early morning light dawned over the basin, the rays of sun cast through the treetops that lined the ridge lines that surrounded us. The other members of the party began to stir from their tents, the morning banter carried on the light breeze down to me, sitting by the lakeside. However, it did not sound nearly as lively as it usually was today. Taking in a deep breath, I stood up and made my way back to the camp.

Upon first glance, I could tell that unease was pervasive amongst them, the most obvious cases being from Heather and Chuck, who seemed to be in deep discussion near the far side of the camp's perimeter. Harvey sat alongside Arnie, the two of which were huddled over a freshly started fire, cooking some sort of delicious stew. Marcus was in conversation with Harlan near his tent, concern on both of their faces. I did not bother looking any further for Jakob as I made my way over to the doctor, the two hushing as I approached.

"Hey, doc. Can I talk to you about something when you have a moment?" I asked. The older man seemed timid and exhausted as he looked up at me. Marcus excused himself to join the two cooks by the fire who were, evidently, having a merry time.

"What seems to be the matter, Samuel?" Harlan asked tiredly.

"I had another one of those dreams..."

His eyes seemed to stare through me for a moment before he snapped back.

"It would seem that you are not the only one," he noted hoarsely. Clearing his throat, he beckoned for me to follow him over to Chuck and Heather.

"Now, I don't normally do this as it violates just about every single code of ethics in psychiatry, but I think we all need to have a conversation about what is going on between you three," Harlan stated, addressing the group gathered around him.

"What I told you earlier is the truth, Harlan," Heather muttered.

Chuck nodded in agreement. "Same here."

The doctor pinched the bridge of his nose between slightly trembling fingers, closing his eyes in frustration.

"This sounds like nothing more than some kind of shared psychosis, whether brought on by conversations you've had together or some kind of illicit substance use. Whatever it is, I need you three to get it under control. I cannot have the trip fall apart when we are this far away from civilization. Even at double speed, we are at least a day and a half away from anyone else."

"But Harlan—" I started before being interrupted by the doctor, who was evidently distraught.

"Whatever it is you all are seeing is nothing. I suggest you drop it before you get the other members of the group freaked out. Paranoia is contagious," he spat harshly before turning away from us. I had never seen this side of him before in my years seeing him, the dramatic and jarring shift in his personality in just the past few days alone being enough to set us over the edge. Without thinking, I grabbed the sleeve of his khaki jacket. He whipped around, glaring at me.

"I can't speak for them, but I do not feel safe here. I think it might be best if we turn back now."

The other two agreed solemnly. The doctor simmered for a moment before tossing his head back so that he faced the sky, letting out a deep, forced sigh that turned into a low growl the longer it went.

"Fine. But when we get back, I expect to see you three back at my office at the earliest possible time so we can address this issue before you all spiral and end up in a mental institution," he muttered, joining the others by the fire. I exchanged a series of worried looks with Heather and Chuck, both of whom appeared exhausted.

"No sleep?" I queried. Chuck yawned and shook his head while Heather made no reaction and acted as though she were lost in another world behind her glazed-over eyes.

"They getting worse for you too?" Chuck asked me after a moment.

"Definitely. I'm also having a harder time telling where the dreams start and end. This can't be a coincidence that all three of us are having similar experiences."

"I shouldn't have told the story by the fire," Heather chimed in, directed at no one in particular.

"I was having these kinds of dreams before I even met you. I don't think what Harlan was saying about this being some kind of 'shared psychosis' is even remotely true. He also just seems off," I said in response.

"Well, I've never had dreams like this before that story, and now I've had them every single night. I'm no psychologist, but maybe the trained professional is on to something here, and we're just getting deeper into our heads about it," Chuck suggested, his frustration thinly masked within a shroud of arrogance. I could tell that he didn't truly believe it, but maybe he was just trying to convince himself of it. He stormed off, making for the woods just beyond the boulders, leaving me with Heather.

"Do you think we should tell anyone else what's going on?" I asked her.

"What good do you think that will bring? I don't agree with Harlan's thoughts on all of this, but he is right about freaking out the others. We are at least twenty miles from town by now, maybe even more. Getting a group of people who are out of their minds coordinated long enough to make that trip back would be next to impossible. I think we best keep this to ourselves," she retorted.

"If there is something going on, wouldn't it be best that they know too? How do we know this is isolated to just us? Marcus didn't look too hot today, either. The spirit of the group is off, and I know you've noticed," I clapped back, trying to keep my voice down while my temper soared. Her face relaxed when I mentioned Marcus, her eyes darting toward the group clustered around the fire. I could hear the conversation shared there, but even without looking, I could tell that he was not involved in the cheery banter between Harvey and Arnie. She returned her gaze back to me, softening.

"I disagree with telling anyone, but you might be right about how everyone has been acting. Aside from Arnie and Harvey, everyone is more on edge now. Hell, I've never seen Harlan get so fired up before, and I've been seeing him for damn near a decade," she paused for a moment, pondering what she would say next, before continuing, "I will talk with Marcus. In the meantime, let's keep this between the three of us until something changes."

Concluding our conversation, we both joined the group by the campfire, helping ourselves to some of the stew that had been prepared. Heather took a seat next to Marcus, where the two of them began talking in hushed voices. Harvey and Arnie were bickering over which local team would win the regional hockey championship and began to solicit the others. It helped dissipate some of the unease I had been feeling prior.

However, this feeling was short-lived when Heather tossed a glance over at me amidst her quiet discussion with Marcus, a grim look plastered on her face. Without exchanging words, I knew that he was having the dreams, too. Harlan must've also noticed as he stood up, clanking his spoon against the metallic bowl he had been eating from.

"Alright, everyone, listen up. There has been an unfortunate change in plans, so we are going to have to cut the trip short. I know this isn't ideal, but we're going to start working our way back. While you all are tearing down camp, I will review the maps to determine the best way to go from here. Dreadfully sorry, but we'll give it another crack next year," the doctor said in a monotone, energy-less voice. He looked over at me through squinting eyes before stepping away from the fire, pulling his map from his jacket breast pocket.

The rest of the group worked hastily to gather the supplies and deconstruct the tents, though it didn't seem as though they had caught on to what was going on. In a way, it almost seemed that a few were relieved to be turning back, perhaps missing the luxuries civilization afforded. Within a matter of no more than fifteen minutes, it was as though we had never been here. We all gathered around

Harlan, who appeared to be in much better spirits now than he had been earlier.

"I have charted us a course back. Due to the nature of the terrain and also wanting to cut down on the overall distance, we will be taking a slightly different path. Everyone ready to go?"

With much-needed enthusiasm, the group set off, following a path alongside the opposite side of the lake, this time so that we were in the shade of the trees that lined the shore. When compared to the other side of the lake, this particular track was significantly more narrow, only allowing us to march in single file. It was wedged between the steep, sloping hillside to our right and an equally precipitous drop to the still water below on our left. After around an hour or so, the trees began to thin out, taking their much-needed shade with them.

Unlike with the days prior, there was very little chatter amongst the party, with much of the enthusiasm from earlier drying up in the scorch of the sun. To continue onward and maintain our momentum, we elected not to stop for lunch, instead choosing to snack on what little remained of the granola. By mid-afternoon, we had reached the other end of the lake after trekking along its edge for a minimum of three hours.

It felt odd to be nearly back to where we had started the day prior, staring up the sloping hills before us to see the grassy meadow with its blossoming flowers waving in the distance. It would've been nice to pass back through there again, but our path did not include that destination. Instead, Harlan led us through a heavily wooded gorge, the Crag perfectly centered between the opposing slopes, its daunting, grey surface sitting ominously against darkening clouds in the sky beyond.

The pass was lined with tangles of roots and walls of rock, gentle trickles of water running down their surfaces so that the area was constantly slick beneath our feet. The ascent was a gradual one as we progressed through the ravine, the dormant volcano growing larger as we drew nearer to its base. Despite still being several miles away from it, I could feel its sinister presence as it loomed before us, and I desperately hoped that we would come no closer to it. Upon exiting the other side of the gorge an hour or so later, and to my dismay, Harlan continued along as if pulled toward it.

"I hate the look of that mountain," Harvey said to me as he came up to my left, not removing his gaze from it.

"It looks unnatural compared to the area around it. It's the tallest thing for miles. Almost feels like it was just put there," I added in agreement. Harvey nodded, smirking.

"Glad I'm not the only one. Ever since Heather's story about that ghost... or whatever it was... I just feel off when I look at it. I know there was some significance to it with the Natives, but I think most of that knowledge is gone now. It's a shame, really..." He trailed off, still focusing on the desolate mountain.

After a moment, he seemed to come to and added, "Any idea why we are turning back?"

I shrugged, attempting to hide that I had any knowledge of the matter, but he saw directly through my facade.

"What aren't you telling me, Sam?" he pressed. I shook my head.

"Nothing! I promise it is nothing," I forced, trying harder to make it convincing. This seemed to work somewhat better, though I knew he doubted it by the way he looked me over afterward. It was some time before we spoke again, and I felt a deep regret for lying to him, but I persuaded myself that it was a necessary evil to keep him safe.

---

We stopped for the night a few hours later, our path having snaked through a few more valleys, which had, thankfully, taken us further away from the Crag. However, its menacing peak still hung over the treetops overhead as we made camp near a cliff face that towered above by perhaps one hundred feet, surrounded by a dense cluster of old pines.

No fire was prepared that night as exhaustion took hold, and the members of the party wanted nothing more than to set up their shelters and fall asleep. I shared a few bites of jerky with Harvey sat atop a fallen log, keeping the conversation casual and lighthearted while we danced around the elephant in the room. It wasn't until we had wrapped up and I stood to make for my tent a few yards away that he loosely took hold of my sleeve.

"Sam. Are we in danger?" he asked, his voice low. I looked down at him in the fading light, holding eye contact with him for a moment while I searched for reassurances I could give him. But none came.

"Honestly? I don't know."

# EIGHT

I laid awake that night, staring up at the seam where the two sides of my tent came together, the faint shimmer of the pine branch shadows cast by the moonlight danced on the orange surface. There was very little preparation that could be done while waiting for sleep to wash over me and the haunting ordeal that would follow. After some time fighting a losing battle, I gave in to the exhaustion and warm embrace of slumber.

Opening my eyes after crossing the veil, I found myself standing before the rope bridge across the river, the waters below unusually still, almost as though time itself had stalled. Above was a brilliantly clear and vibrant night sky with more stars than I could possibly have imagined there ever being. And, unlike past nights, I was engulfed in the sounds of insects and the gentle rustling of trees in the soft breeze. Seeing no immediate threat, I lowered my guard and breathed deeply, giving myself a moment of respite.

Once I felt well enough to determine my next course of action, I noticed movement in my peripheral vision across the river. To my surprise, a figure emerged: a figure of an old man. As he drew closer to the other end of the rope bridge, I could make out the distinctive features of my father, with his battered work overalls and flannel shirt.

"Dad!" I exclaimed as he came to a stop just beyond the wooden anchor poles. He waved me over, to which I promptly obliged, crossing the bridge with haste. When I reached the other side, I embraced him with all of the strength I could muster. He smelled of tobacco and cut grass, though it seemed to fade the longer I was there. Pulling away, I said, "I'm so happy I can see you again."

"I am too, son. I have been trying to get back to you. We were unable to finish our talk last time, and I was worried I had let you down," he returned, a warmth in his gruff voice but also concern buried just below the surface.

"What about it? Do you know something about what's been going on?" I asked, trying my best not to let the bubbling fear in the pit of my stomach grow.

"I don't know how much more help I can be for you. I feel my strength faltering. But this is a warning. Something terrible has happened, I know it. Nothing more can be done for him, but *you* still have a chance. You must do whatever it takes to escape," he said sternly.

"Dad, I—"

He interrupted me, suddenly pulling me back into a strong hug, feeling him quietly sob and shudder.

"I am sorry I couldn't be there for you. I failed you as a father, and I never got the chance to try and make it better. You are facing something that we all must face, alone, because I wasn't there, and I don't know that I can be now. Just know that I love you, and I hope that you can forgive me," he whimpered between shallow breaths. In my whole life, I had only ever seen this man cry once, on my wedding day, and I pitied him for always having to hold any emotion in for the sake of maintaining some notion of stability or strength.

"I love you too, dad. I should've let you in. I'm sorry I wasted the time we had. You don't have to seek forgiveness from me. If anything, I should be the one begging for yours," I responded, tears streaming down my cheeks. I could feel his arms loosening and his body pulling away.

"I have to go now. This is no place for me, but I had to do what I could to see you one last time. What happens next is for you, and you alone, to determine. In the end, we all travel the same road," he spoke, his words cold and haunting. Without warning, he simply vanished before me, fading into wisps of thin smoke that drifted into the heavens above. I collapsed to my knees, crying out as I gasped for air, pounding the dirt with a clenched fist until it became numb. Sobbing for minutes or hours, I could not tell, only that I felt an emptiness within and a solitude like no other.

Somewhere beyond me, in the dark, a twig snapped underfoot. And then another, followed by another, drawing closer each time. I clambered to my feet, heart pounding, rubbing my eyes and readjusting my vision. Through the tears, I saw the silhouette of the gaunt figure from the past nights, though it was much larger now, with spiny protrusions along its shoulders and back, hunched over on all fours, with razor-like talons that dug into the damp soil. It let out a moan that sounded as though it were comprised of two different, dissonant voices, both fighting each other for dominance as they leaped from its throat.

We stared at each other for what felt like ages, neither of us making a move. In the pale, dying light of the moon above, I could just barely read its features, but I could see that it appeared to be smiling at me with sharp teeth behind thin lips that curled back from its mouth, unable to contain its gaping maw. I thought I saw its tongue dance around in the blackness, but I did not want to linger any longer. It shifted its weight, clicking its teeth, a low drone—or growl—gurgling up from within its throat, sunken, dead eyes resting squarely on me.

As it began to lumber forward, I raced for the bridge again, barreling across it, my vision blurring and the muted colors of my surroundings melding into each other. Tossing a glance over my shoulder as I reached the other side, I noticed it was gone. All that remained was a heavy presence that hung in the still, cool air, like an omnipresent sense of one's personal dread. I hunched over, catching my breath, heaving deep gasps until my lungs felt sore. That was the closest I had ever been to it. *What on earth was it, and what was my father trying to share?* I thought to myself. *None of this makes any sense.*

I truly felt more lost and alone than I had ever felt before.

---

I WAS JOLTED awake by the sound of bone-chilling screaming emanating from somewhere beyond the bounds of my tent. Without thinking, I tore through the membrane as quickly as I could manage, assessing what was occurring. The group had gathered around the tattered remains of the doctor's abode, the tendrils of loose, blue fabric fluttering in the breeze. Racing over to them, I found Arnie on his knees, hands clasped over his ghastly white face, wailing uncontrollably. Heather had crouched down beside him, wrapping her arms around him in an attempt to ease and comfort, but it seemed to be in vain. Coming to stand alongside the bulwark that was Harvey, his arms crossed and face furrowed into deep concern, I examined the mangled mess before us.

If I hadn't known it was previously a tent, I doubt I would've been able to guess now. The sides had been ripped apart with long gashes that ran the lengths of the walls, cut with immense strength and razor-sharp accuracy, like a hot knife through butter left out in the sun. Inside, a bloody, putrid mess of clothes and general camping supplies lie scattered in the interior. But there was no sign of the doctor himself and not a single track or footprint that led away from the site of the massacre. It was as though the assailant had simply vanished along with its victim.

"...what... what could do something like this?" Arnie gasped between sobs, his round body trembling as he struggled to regain his composure.

"Bear, maybe? Ya'll have bears up here, right? Grizzlies?" Jakob prodded, perhaps a little too nonchalantly considering the situation. "Good thing I brought my gun."

"They are incredibly rare in these parts. Besides, look around you. Do you see any tracks?" Chuck responded his words dripping with disgust and disdain, likely directed at his brother's lack of conscience. Jakob shifted his weight, eyeing the surrounding forest floor, shaking his head as he lowered his gaze to his feet, defeated. The older Washburn exhaled sharply, "That's what I thought."

"Whatever it was, it had to have been huge. Look at the markings on the tent and the angle it cut from. The thing would've been at least ten feet tall. Does anything get that big around here?" Marcus observed, his voice shaky, a few of the words catching awkwardly in his throat.

"We're all going to die!" exclaimed Arnie, suddenly, cracking. Heather shushed him.

"Something that big, we should've heard—especially if

it had attacked Harlan. I mean, just look at this," I interjected, gesturing widely to the scene. "There is no way he just silently took this, and nobody else heard it. Hell, you Washburns are set up less than—what—ten feet away?"

Everyone's eyes turned and fell upon the brothers, who looked around in bewilderment, Chuck scoffing as though he were insulted by the insinuation.

"I am a notoriously light sleeper. I would've heard this happening. You can't seriously think we had any part in this, can you?" Chuck hissed. Jakob was glaring at the rest of us as he turned around, making for the tent they shared, returning seconds later with his rifle slung over his shoulder. I couldn't tell if it was meant as intimidation or not.

"We have to go looking for him. He's our ticket out of here," Harvey piped up, startling me with his booming voice.

"Bad idea. If there is a wild animal out there, it will likely come back. Our best bet is to stay together," Chuck protested. The two men remained silent for a moment, glaring at each other with tension palpable enough to cut.

"So your plan is to sit around and do nothing while a friend is out there, dying?" Harvey asked, his voice trembling under great restraint as his face grew more red by the second. I had never seen him angry before, and it was both unsettling and terrifying at the same time. Chuck exhaled sharply, pointing back at the bloodied tent.

"Harlan is already dead. What makes you think he could lose that much blood and still be alive? Let alone the objective truth that if a wild animal did attack him unprovoked, it was likely hungry. There is no point in risking anyone else on what could prove to be a suicide mission."

"And who on earth put you in charge, Chuck?" demanded Heather, still trying to calm down Arnie.

"I just did," he retorted. Suddenly, there was a violent uproar between the members of the group, their individual voices drowned out in the cacophony of shouting. Jakob had unslung his rifle, holding it in both hands, the veins in his neck protruding with the force at which he roared.

"Will you all—please—just shut the hell up for one goddamn second!" Heather shouted, somehow defeating the voices of the others. The camp fell silent as she glared around us. "Thank you. Now, Chuck is probably right, Harvey. I don't think there would be much left to save of poor, old Harlan. However, Harvey does have a point. We have no idea where we are or how to get out of here—"

"We can just use his maps," sneered Chuck, beckoning to the carnage. Heather let out a sarcastic chuckle.

"Be my guest. Now, while science boy over here looks for the maps, I think we need to establish a plan. I am not volunteering to lead—I do not want to, but I refuse to let testosterone junkies get us all killed because you can't swallow your pride for ten seconds to realize we are all in danger now. Sam? You've been quiet. What do you think?"

The words struck me by surprise, and my voice caught in my dry throat.

"We should take stock of supplies. Make sure the thing didn't get into anything else. Maybe try to pinpoint where exactly we are so the maps will be useful?" I said. Heather thoughtfully tapped her chin with the index finger on her right hand, glancing up into the early morning sky. Following her gaze, I noticed the crimson coloring of the clouds ominously looming overhead, leaving me deeply unsettled and a haunting sense of forlorn in my chest. She clapped her hands together, causing me to jump a little where I stood.

"Good ideas. I want you and Harvey checking the

vicinity of the camp. Look for any signs of the animal. Chuck—Jakob—you two are on map-finding duty. Marcus—you're going to help me and Arnie check our supplies. I want everyone back here in fifteen minutes."

With a new sense of urgency, the group broke ranks, skittering away in various directions as each person worked on their initiative. The two Washburn brothers rummaged through the bloody mess of rags and flesh, searching for any sign of the doctor's maps and other directional instruments. I followed Harvey away from the others, his broad shoulders fixed and arms barely moving as he marched. I could tell he was still fuming.

"The Washburns are pretty thick-skulled, aren't they?" I joked, attempting to dispel the tension that loomed in the air around us. Harvey let out a deep, long sigh, a light chuckle following shortly afterward, though he did not respond. After we had made our way down the shallow rise and out of earshot of the others, he stopped and turned to me.

"I asked you if we were in danger, Sam. I didn't believe you then, I still don't believe you now. We are miles away from any semblance of civilization, and someone is likely dead. I need you to be honest with me. What is going on?"

I hesitated, staring into his questioning eyes, but the remainder of his features were stark and hardened, devoid of any emotion.

"I don't know what is going on. I don't know what happened to the doctor—"

"I heard you three talking with Harlan yesterday. I couldn't make out all of it, but you sounded pretty frustrated with him. Something about dreams—or nightmares," he said in a monotone voice, drawing closer to me in a vaguely intimidating way. I backed up, finding myself caught against the trunk of a pine tree.

"I *swear* I didn't do anything. I have no idea what is going on. We've been having these dreams and begged him to turn us around. We were heading back because he was worried we were going crazy—you've got to believe me," I pleaded. He stopped progressing toward me, his face softening.

"Never crossed my mind. Someone as scrawny as you wouldn't be able to do that. I just needed to know that you weren't aware of what *might've* done it." He reached down and pulled me off of the tree, resin and needles stuck to the back of my flannel. "What are these dreams?"

"To be honest, I don't really know. I've been having odd ones for years now, pretty much ever since my wife passed and I moved here, but something has changed. The most recent ones have me trapped in these woods with this thing —this creature—hunting me like it's some kind of game—or worse. I always seem to wake up before it gets to me, though. I don't want to know what happens if it gets to me," I explained with a shaky sigh, avoiding eye contact with Harvey, who listened intently.

"So you've had them every night we've been out here? Is that why you were acting off after the first day?" he asked, genuine concern in his voice, leaving me wishing I hadn't told him. Seeing that there was no way out of the pit I dug myself into, I nodded, confirming his suspicions. Even then, he still seemed baffled, like a child witnessing a crude magic trick at a traveling carnival. "Why didn't you tell me sooner? I thought there was something I did that made you upset."

"Because I didn't want you to think I was completely insane. I'm definitely not all right in the head—haven't been for a long time now—and you are the first real friend I've had in years that didn't pity me or indulge me in my sadness." I let out a sigh, craning my head to the clouds above. "I just don't understand why this is happening to me."

Harvey unexpectedly embraced me with such force that any air I had left in my lungs was quickly expelled. "Life can be a tricky thing, but there is no one that can do it all alone. Thank you for talking to me," he expressed, releasing me. I stood there for a moment, drifting back to the same embrace I had shared with my father during my last dream, willing myself not to completely break down under the weight of how alone I truly felt. Instead, I thanked Harvey for understanding and being a friend I could rely on, avowing that I would share the truth from now on. This seemed to be enough for him.

Together, we continued around the perimeter of the camp, just below the rise it had been set upon. Coming around a thicket of spiny underbrush, I found myself alone. Glancing around for Harvey, my gaze came to a rest on a hollow in the sheer wall of rock the camp had been set up against—a cave of sorts, its black, shadowy maw oddly alluring. I crept toward it, hearing what sounded like a steady trickle of water reverberating from within the emptiness.

As I drew closer, I noticed that the rhythm matched the beat of my heart, increasing as the realization dawned. But, by now, I was being drawn in by some machinations beyond my control—I could not stop my own two feet. Soon, I was standing at the edge, peering into the impenetrable void that seemed to hungrily swallow up the early morning light. Listening to the mesmerizing, rhythmic drum of the trickling water somewhere in the depths, I thought I could make out something else. The more I focused on it, the clearer it became—"*you*"—repeated over and over, just above the volume of a whisper. I could feel the chill climbing my spine and my stomach turn, the hairs on the back of my neck slowly standing up. It was then that I realized the trickle of water was no longer present, just the bodiless *"you"* now. Some of the clouds overhead broke, allowing more sunlight to penetrate the darkness, revealing the face of the creature mere inches from my own, hiding just beyond the murky veil.

I reeled back, tripping over myself and crashing to the forest floor. Scrambling to get back on my unstable feet, I crawled several feet away, my heart pounding in my chest to the point where I swore it might give out entirely. When I turned back, it was no longer there, replaced with the steady trickle of water—the echoing beat in the blackness no longer finding any rhythm.

Picking the dark orange pine needles off of my flannel and brushing the dirt from my pants, I found my head spinning and mind writhing. *Am I even awake right now? How do I know that this isn't still a dream?* I held up one of the needle clusters, bending its brittle structures to the point of snapping. I snagged another, pricking myself in the palm of my hand. *This is real,* I determined, watching a small bead of crimson blood well up from the puncture wound. Wiping it off on my pants, I began marching back toward the voices of the others. Coming over the rise, Harvey swooped in.

"Where'd you get off to? One second, you're beside me. The next, you're just gone," he exclaimed, his concern masked by a layer of humor.

"I actually found something interesting back that way," I responded, thumbing in the direction of the cave where the thing had been lurking. "Some sort of cave. I didn't go in, though."

"Think the animal went in there? I'm willing to bet that

Jakob is itching to shoot something. Probably don't even need to tell him anything else," he chuckled, the unease still evident in his voice and mannerisms.

"We'll let the group know, and they can decide what to do from there, I guess."

Together, we returned to the camp where the group had already begun to loosely assemble around Heather.

"Alright. I'm going to do this once and only this once. Status reports—Marcus?" she shouted, carrying in her voice something I could not quite put my finger on. *This almost sounds 'army,'* I considered, my mind churning through potential ideas. It made me realize just how little I knew about her after spending the last several days together.

"I'm not sure how much we had before, but we've got at least three more days of food. Might have to start rationing. We are running low on clean water," Marcus returned timidly—a shell of his former, vibrant self.

"Chuck—Jakob—what did you find?"

"No maps and no compass," the older Washburn said, a twinge of defeat in his still-arrogant tone. Jakob shifted his rifle uneasily as the eyes of the group drifted to them.

"He kept those in his jacket. No sign of it?" Heather pressed. They both shook their heads in unison.

"Negative. Just some of his shirt and sleeping bag. We did find this, though..." Chuck lifted up a battered and bloody, leather-bound book—perhaps a journal.

"Anything helpful in there?" she asked, reaching her open hand out. He placed it in her palm, gently and hesitantly, almost as though it carried immense weight and significance.

"The last entry..."

She began reading aloud, "August 4th. The others are starting to notice that something is up. Washburn, Stratton, and Prichard are seeing it too. It almost got me last night. I followed the road home, but it was behind me. I could smell its decaying breath outside the door before it came in through the window. If it wasn't for my alarm waking me up, I am sure it would've had me. I am leading the party back now. I don't think they know yet. We've got to get out of this forest and back across the river. It is coming."

Nobody spoke for several minutes as Heather closed the journal and tucked it into a pocket in her jeans. The silence drew out, only occasionally interrupted by the sound of distant birdsong or the hammering of a woodpecker from somewhere far away. The forest was deadly quiet and lifeless here in such a way that it left me feeling uncomfortable.

"Heather? What did Harlan mean?" Arnie cautiously inquired from behind Marcus. "What are you seeing?"

She ignored him for a moment, locking eyes with me, asking, "What did you and Harvey find?"

---

THE GROUP GATHERED around the black opening into the cliffside that I had found minutes prior, a growing sense of dread welling up in my chest again. Standing aside, I watched as Heather stepped forward, peering into the nothingness beyond. By now, a new sensation was arising—a foul, musty smell that seemed to emanate from the opening.

"Think it went in there? We got it cornered!" Jakob exclaimed excitedly, unslinging the rifle from his shoulder and bolting the action. Harvey nudged me with his elbow.

"Told you," he whispered.

"And what do you think you're going to try and do?" Heather interrogated as the eager Washburn drew closer.

"Well, ain't it obvious? That animal probably set up

shop in there. We kill it, and we find the maps. Two birds, one stone," he responded, trying to push past Heather, who was now actively blocking his path.

"That has got to be the dumbest thing I have ever heard someone say, and I have heard some pretty dumb shit in my time. Back off before you get yourself killed," she cracked, audibly and visibly agitated.

"Looks like a mineshaft," Chuck interjected helplessly. We all turned toward him expectantly. "This area used to be big on gold back in the day. There were hundreds of illegal mining operations set up back in the 1870s. I did a whole segment on it a few years ago..." He trailed off, his arrogance seemingly having evaporated completely. I could tell that his cavalier attitude was merely a facade and had now worn off at the realization that he could not talk his way out of what was coming—the inevitability of fear and the stark gravity of the danger we all now faced.

"Man-made or not, I am going in there and killing it," Jakob persisted, his temper flaring.

"Hot-headed as always—" Heather started before being violently thrust aside by the Washburn, readying his rifle. At that, Harvey and I rushed forward, grabbing him by the shoulder and arms, respectively. He whipped around the butt of his weapon and rammed it into Harvey's face, sending him flailing backward. At that point, I was seeing red—and an opportunity to let out the pent-up rage I felt toward this sorry excuse for a man.

I landed several well-placed punches on his face and stomach, and my time as a competing boxer in college came back to me. I was rusty, but he was stunned by the flurry of quick attacks. Unfortunately, he shifted his stance and brought the stock of the rifle up into my chest, knocking the wind from my lungs. With the rage piling on, I grabbed him by the neck, bringing the much larger man to the ground, colliding his thick skull against some loose stones at the opening of the cave. I squeezed, feeling his heartbeat as my grip tightened around his throat—the world around me disappearing into a fog as I watched him struggle to break free.

*"you... you... you..."* The cave spoke to me as it had before, its words matching the pounding of my heart. *"... you... kill."* I looked up, and, for a split second, I thought I saw the glimmer of its teeth from somewhere within—smiling.

By then, both Heather and Harvey were on me, pulling me away from Jakob, who was now heaving strenuously as he rolled back and forth, gasping for air that was too slow to come. He was still hacking and wheezing as Heather snatched his rifle from the ground, tossing it to Harvey, who awkwardly stood to the side, unsure of how to handle the machine.

"I pegged you for smarter, Sam. Damn good job," she said coldly and sarcastically, holding the collar of my shirt in a white-knuckle grip. The rush of rage and adrenaline had worn off now, and the realization of what I had just done was settling in. *I was going to kill him, wasn't I? Did it want me to?*

"Out of my way—out of my way!" Jakob was shouting as he stood back up, his voice hoarse. Harvey wrapped a large hand around the younger Washburn's shoulder, holding him in place. "I'm going to end you, Stratton!"

"Now, will everyone just shut up?" Heather barked, perhaps more annoyed than angry, but I could not tell. I was still grappling with what I had done—what I had *almost* done.

"Calm down, Jakob. You're getting yourself worked up,"

Chuck ordered, glaring at his brother. The younger one scoffed.

"He was going to kill me! That *freak* was going to kill me," he pleaded, sounding more and more like a child whose parents didn't buy them a toy at the store and decided to throw a tantrum. The older Washburn tossed a disapproving glance my way before addressing his sibling again.

"If we're being fair, you started it. Like usual," he said disdainfully. "Ma would be real disappointed in you right now—trying to throw yourself away by going into an abandoned mineshaft and dying—not to mention they were only trying to stop you until you decided it was best to attack them."

He turned toward Heather. "I want you to hold onto the gun. Keep it out of *his* hands before he has any more brilliant ideas. I was slow on the uptake, but I know a jarhead when I see one. I think you are in a much better position to handle that."

"Former."

Heather fell silent, seeming much smaller now. She slackened her hold on my shirt and took the gun from Harvey, much to the vocal dismay of Jakob, who was seething at the thought of being stripped of his only power. And then his gaze fell on me—a combination of hatred and envy in his eyes.

"All in favor of Ms. Prichard leading from here on?" Chuck queried, addressing the group. Slowly but surely, the others began to raise their hands in silent agreement. He smiled and said, "I guess that settles it then."

"What are we doing now?" Harvey asked reluctantly.

"We're going to pack up what's left of camp and make for higher ground. We need to know our cardinal directions before we do anything else," Heather responded stoically. I could see the Marine in her now, but I wondered why she would withhold that detail and why she was so opposed to leading the rest of the group.

---

It was several hours later when we came to a halt near the top of a bald hill, the thin brush and young trees indicating that it was likely the subject of a small fire at one point in the not-so-distant past, the afternoon sun hanging overhead. The group broke ranks and split into separate pods, each occupying shade beneath the few trees that remained that offered a reprieve from the oppressive heat. Heather bounced between each smaller group—first starting with Marcus and Arnie—then Chuck and Jakob—before finally arriving at myself and Harvey.

"So what now?" Harvey asked as she drew closer. This was the first time he had spoken since the incident earlier that day.

"We need to wait a little while. The group needs a break, and we have to wait for the sun to start coming down some more. Unfortunately, we got up here about the same time as noon, so the shadows can't tell us East from West. We'll give it an hour. By then, I should have a better idea of where we need to head. In the meantime, drink up and stay hydrated. This is one of those rare days where there are no clouds," she advised. We both nodded, and she left to go sit with Marcus and Arnie about twenty-odd feet away.

"So, are we going to talk about what happened?" Harvey asked me abruptly through the awkward tension.

"I don't know that there is much to talk about. He attacked you and Heather, and I've had a bone to pick with him since before we even set out on this hike. Combine that with the sleep deprivation, and I think I just kind of snapped."

"You weren't going to kill him, though, right?" he pressed.

I paused for a second, unsure how I should proceed, searching for a political answer that would both suffice and also not confirm that I was—indeed—going to kill him.

"I... I was going to stop. I just had to make sure first is all." This seemed to do well enough for Harvey as he nodded solemnly.

"Do you think what got Harlan was actually in there?"

"I wouldn't rule it out, no. But Chuck is right; going in there would've been suicidal. I don't know much about those mines, but they have these dead zones where no oxygen can get to them, and you just suffocate—and that's excluding the hundred-foot drops covered by century-old wood boards," I responded.

"Was it wrong to just leave his stuff there like that, though? No service or nothing—just a pile of bloody trash somewhere in the middle of the wilderness?" Harvey asked though I wondered if it was more a question to himself. "I did not expect this trip to turn out like this. Never, in a million years, would I have guessed it would go this badly..." he trailed off, lost in thought.

"Me neither," I added, but I doubted he was still listening.

"I'm worried that I'm never going to see my wife again, Sam. I'm worried she's going to have to raise our son or daughter without me. I tried to be better—give more than I took, you know? And this is how it all ended up. Stuck on the side of some damned hill, waiting to die."

I could tell he was on the verge of tears now, barely

holding them back. We sat there in silence for a while longer, listening to the sound of the wind battering against the hillside and smelling the sweet scent of pine that it carried. In the distance, I could see the lake nestled in the basin where we had stayed just the day earlier, wishing I could go back to before this nightmare became all too real.

# NINE

After several more hours of hiking, the group came to a stop nestled in a narrow valley between steep slopes that ascended to either side, leaving me feeling as though we were walled in. Harvey and I set up our tents next to each other near the bank of a gentle brook, finding a suitable patch of dirt amongst the loose stones. We hadn't spent much time with the others the remainder of the day, instead choosing to keep to ourselves as much as possible. I purposefully avoided any sort of eye contact with Jakob, though I could often feel his gaze burning into the back of my skull like a red hot, branding iron—marking me for the slaughter. I regretted my actions, but a part of me, deep down, regretted not going even further. And that was the part that scared me the most.

Sat on a few larger rocks, I shared a bite to eat with Harvey—a concoction of assorted, salted nuts and stale oats. Even with his imposing exterior, I could tell that something had snapped in the poor man since this morning. His stature seemed diminished, almost to the point that it was like a child wearing clothes that were too big. I wondered if he would ever talk to me again if we made it out of here alive.

Clearing the thought from my mind, I finished my meal and thanked Harvey for sharing with me, making a joke about not wanting to eat dry cereal again. As I was standing up, I felt the burning sensation of being watched. Slowly turning around, I expected to see the younger Washburn, only to be surprised by Arnie sitting on a rocky outcrop near the edge of the camp's perimeter, partially hidden by the long shadows cast by the setting sun. I cautiously waved, thinking that maybe he was either spaced out or had been waiting to get my attention, but he made no reaction—he simply continued starting, a blank expression plastered on his round face.

"Need something?" I called out. He cocked his head to one side as though I addressed him in a foreign tongue that he did not understand.

"No, I'm okay," he responded after a moment of unsettling silence. I nodded anxiously before ducking into my tent and sealing it off from the rest of the world. *Well, that was not normal,* I thought to myself, a chill running down the length of my spine. *Should I go tell Heather? No, that would just get people worked up. Arnie is just out of it after what happened today.* Convincing myself that nothing more needed to be done, I climbed into my sleeping bag and waited for some semblance of sleep to wash over me, praying that I would not have to face *it* tonight.

---

THE RELIEF from my exhaustion was a hard-fought battle that I was beginning to think I could not win, with thoughts of everything that had transpired in the past few days rushing around inside my mind, reminding me that what was happening was all too real. I tried every trick I had read about, from holding my breath to counting backward from one hundred, all of which failed to calm my nerves enough to sleep. But every time I closed my eyes, I could see *its* face staring back at me from within the darkness, the gray skin stretched so thinly around the bone that it seemed as though it could tear with the slightest touch, its sunken and dead eyes, meeting mine.

I was startled when I thought I heard a voice, no more than a whisper in the wind, calling my name. Initially, I tried to persuade myself that it was just a gentle breeze rushing down through the valley, but it became clearer the more I focused on it. Against my better judgment, I got up and exited the tent. It's not like the thin fabric would've protected against much anyway.

The air outside was surprisingly cold, making me second-guess my decisions. But before I could return to the relative warmth and safety of the tent, I noticed that Arnie was standing in the same place he was before, watching me just at the bounds of the moonlight near the edge of the camp, his back against a wall of darkness and the thick of the forest beyond. I could feel my heartbeat quickening.

"Hey Arnie..." There was no response, just a continuation of the burning, haunting gaze. I reluctantly drew a few steps closer.

"Are you okay? I can go get Heather or Marcus if you don't want to talk to me." He began speaking, but no audible words passed his lips. Just silence.

"I don't know what you're saying. Here, why don't you and I go get Heather—"

Before I could finish my sentence, his small body burst open, sending viscera and blood in every direction for several feet—what little remaining of his frame collapsing to the ground. It twitched and writhed in the crimson pool for several excruciating seconds as I watched helplessly, my voice caught in my throat as I tried to call for help.

"It's coming, Sam," a familiar, smooth voice said from behind. Whirling around, I made out the pale figure of Harlan, nearly opaque in the moonlight.

"What's going on? What happened to you?" I demanded, trying to keep the growing fear from my trembling voice. He smiled.

"A chain of events has been set into motion. The world's deadliest predator is coming for you."

"I need you to tell me what I can do to stop it," I insisted desperately.

"You can't stop it, Sam. Many before you have tried and failed. No one has ever survived. You can't delay what's inevitable," he uttered his tone an unnerving combination of pleasantness and ominous. Before I could continue pressing him, I felt something warm trickling around my bare feet. Looking down, I realized it was Arnie's blood that had slowly seeped away from his ruptured corpse a few feet away, the trail meandering toward the stream. When I looked up again, the doctor was nowhere to be found, having disappeared into the enveloping dark.

I followed the sanguine river down to the water's edge, staring down into the blackness, its glasslike surface completely still. Without putting too much thought into why a flowing brook would have stopped, I dipped my blood-soaked foot into its depths, sending ripples running outward in concentric rings. And then, from within the murky blackness, a skeletal, claw-like hand caught hold of my ankle, pulling with enough force to send me crashing onto my rear.

It was squeezing with enough pressure that I was sure it would break my leg in two, tearing my foot cleanly from my body. I writhed, trying to pry away from its iron grip—but it only continued to constrict, pulling me further into the water. Panicking, I started whipping loose stones as hard as I could at the thing lurking below the surface. With luck, I felt it shudder, and its hold temporarily slackened. I repeated my actions with greater precision—the fear changing to dauntless resistance—realizing that I was actively fighting for my life and I would not let it take me.

After a few more solid connections, it let go, retracting the hand back into the water, which immediately began flowing once more. The world around me came to life again as the sounds of the forest returned, a jarring juxtaposition when compared to the eerie quietness I hadn't noticed moments prior. Exhausted, I slumped backward, resting my head against a dirt embankment, drifting to sleep.

---

When I finally awoke, it was to the thrashing of my body by Harvey, who loomed overhead, partially obscuring the early morning sun. *Had I somehow fallen asleep here?* He shook me again, worry plastered clearly all over his face. I started to sit up, the dirt from the embankment crumbling down my shoulders as I did so. Shifting my legs, I winced as a sharp pain shot up from my ankle like lightning. I glanced down and noticed it was heavily bruised. Harvey was also looking at it.

"What the hell happened last night?" he asked, concern practically oozing from his voice.

"What do you mean?" I returned, pulling myself up to my feet, nursing my injured ankle.

"Arnie's gone... and you're just out here with a sprained ankle or something," Harvey said briefly. "We spent fifteen minutes looking for you as well."

Peering back up over the embankment, I scanned for the last place I had seen Arnie last night, my gaze coming to a rest at the rocky outcrop. To my relief, there was no body nor the stain of blood. Harvey swung one of my arms over his shoulder and helped me back up to the camp where the others had all gathered.

"I found him!" Harvey bellowed, his strong voice echoing against the narrow valley walls. Heather rushed over, the rifle carried in one hand. She quickly examined me before coming to a stop at my ankle.

"What happened?" she demanded.

"I had another dream—well, at least I think it was. Arnie..." I started before losing my words.

"Spit it out."

I could tell Heather was deeply worried behind the stoic facade she put up.

"He died. Just sort of exploded before my eyes. Then I saw Harlan. He was speaking in gibberish—I have no idea what he was trying to say. Then I went to go wash off my foot, and *it* tried to pull me into the stream," I finished, emotionless.

"What did the doctor say?" Heather pressed.

"Something about the world's deadliest predator coming to get us and that we couldn't stop it." I listened as his haunting words repeated in my mind like a ghostly whisper at the edge of consciousness. Heather simply stared at me.

"Great—what're we up against? A damn mountain lion?" Jakob shouted ruefully. Chuck shoved him hard with his elbow, silencing him.

"What about Arnie?"

"Oh god. He just exploded. It was horrifying!" I exclaimed, forcing myself not to relive the event to avoid losing my stomach. Heather and Harvey both shuddered at the mention of it, the smirk fading from Jakob's childish face.

"Where did this happen, Sam?" Heather asked painfully. I pointed to the same rocky outcrop a couple of yards away. With the aid of Harvey, the three of us approached slowly, the others trailing behind. As we drew closer, I noticed a series of deep gouges in the stone—heavily mimicking claw marks. The others saw it, too, as they came to an abrupt halt just at the edge of the grass. Nestled compactly between the markings was a single phrase carved into the stone: *it comes for all*.

---

"'What' comes? The animal that is picking us off one by one now? If ya'll had just let me get it, Arnie would still be here," Jakob protested, vying for his rifle again. The group erupted into incoherent shouting as everyone turned on each other. It was quickly put to an end with the crack of gunfire.

"Quiet! All of you shut the hell up!" Heather belted, the rifle—pointed at the sky—still smoking. "Now, I want us to break up into two groups. We're going to find Arnie, and then we are going to continue heading southwest. We've got twenty minutes. Make it count," she barked.

"But what happens if we don't find him?" Marcus asked timidly. His body looked frail, almost corpse-like, with pale skin and tired eyes. Heather just stared at him silently, shaking her head.

"We're burning precious daylight. Marcus—I want you with Sam and Harvey. I'm going with the Washburns. We're all back here in twenty, got it?"

The group nodded and split appropriately, Marcus slowly walking over to Harvey and me with a blank expression on his face. The three of us exchanged no words as we moved up the valley in the opposite direction of the other team, who proceeded down the way we had come yesterday, disappearing into the tangle of underbrush.

We marched silently for several moments, everyone keeping their head on a swivel, scanning the area for signs of Arnie. As we approached the crest of a small rise, Harvey dropped to his knees, brushing away loose pine needles and twigs. We crouched around him to see what he had discovered. Buried partially below the refuse of the forest floor was one of Arnie's hiking boots, torn completely along one side by something razor-sharp. Lifting it to get a better view in the dim light that penetrated the blankets of branches overhead, we noticed it was caked in dried blood mixed with dirt.

"Arnie? Arnie!" Marcus called out hopelessly, cupping his hands around his mouth. Harvey and I exchanged nervous glances before taking hold of Marcus' shoulder.

"I don't think we should be so loud, Marcus. He's gone. And—whatever it is—it's still out there. We should head back to the others and let them know what we found," I said to him, his arms dropping to his sides in defeat as he lowered his head. The quiet walk back to camp was interrupted by an occasional whimper as he sobbed silently behind us.

The others were waiting for us when we entered the clearing, their heads immediately swinging in our direction, briefly illuminated with hopeful expressions that were dashed a second later when they noticed the ravaged boot hanging loosely by the laces in Harvey's hand. Heather approached Marcus and embraced him, sharing a few hushed words as the two mourned the loss of their friend. In that moment, I wished I could've done more somehow—watching their colleague die so violently and being so helpless as to prevent it.

Without any further discussion or orders, the group broke apart, making for their tents to be deconstructed as we prepared to move out. After a few moments, all that remained was the vibrant green shelter that had previously belonged to Arnie, sitting somberly, alone against the backdrop of the stream and forest. It was almost peaceful.

"I'll see you on the other side, my friend," I heard Marcus mutter in its direction as we pressed onward, up the valley once more.

---

THE VALLEY LED us up a winding channel walled on either side by steep slopes that ran up to precipitous summits, the tops of which seemed to disappear into the low-hanging clouds that clung to their invisible peaks. Everything around us felt devoid of life, gray and desolate, reminding me of a time when I lived in a large city with miles and miles of asphalt and concrete, blank faces of others who you had to convince yourself that they were human. I had always hated it—being surrounded on all sides by others but always feeling so uncontrollably and unfathomably alone.

There was very little in the way of vegetation where we were now, what little remaining being mostly comprised of long grasses and the occasional stunted pine tree that was gnarled by the wind that would undoubtedly whip through this passage during storms. The stream had become no more than a gentle trickle of water running freely in the battered stone, carving out its path over the course of eons.

The gradual rise of the valley had brought us up to its highest place, giving us a vantage point to assess our progress. Much to my dismay, we had drawn much closer to the Crag, its proximity previously hidden by the steep walls that had engulfed us for the majority of the day. Dark clouds seemed to circle its dismal peak like vultures circling a corpse. If I had to estimate how close we were to it now, I would've said its base was less than a mile away, perhaps even closer. It was difficult to put a number to it when the low-rising hills nearer to the mountain seemed to undulate like waves on a green ocean.

"That's not looking good, is it?" Heather asked as she turned to Chuck.

"Huh? Oh, you mean the clouds?" the older Washburn responded, surveying the sky. "Not good at all. More rain at best."

"Where are we going to go? We're exposed up here, and that ranger cabin is miles away even if we could find our way back now," Marcus cried out in frustration. It was the first I had heard him speak since that morning. There was a low rumble of thunder somewhere in the distance.

"If that's an actual storm, I don't think the tents are going to cut it. We need to find hard shelter and fast," Harvey added.

"Look over there!" Jakob shouted, pointing at what resembled a scar in the forest—a deep gash where the tree line abruptly ceased and circled—no more than a few hundred yards away. Nestled in the middle of the opening, what appeared to be a wooden tower adorned with a cross reached for the sky. *A church?* I asked myself. *What on earth would a church be doing out here?* There came another crack of thunder, still lingering in the distance, but it could've been closer this time, I could not tell.

"Is that a church?" I asked.

"Might be! Could be an old mining settlement," Chuck speculated with excitement.

"Alright. We're going to scope the place out, but that might be as far as we get today. The clouds are making it difficult to tell which direction the shadows are pointing, and the storm will definitely make traveling dangerous. Now, I want a tight formation. We're going to be moving quickly," she started before turning to me. "Sam, how is your leg? Good to move fast?"

"I can keep up," I confirmed.

"Good, because I don't want to carry you," Harvey whispered, leaning over my shoulder. He let out a slight chuckle, but it was a shell of what I had been used to prior to the events that had unfolded.

Heather barked a few more orders, placing myself and Harvey at the rear of the pack, Marcus in front of us, and the Washburns in front of him. With our reorganized formation and a reinvigorated spirit, we set off down the sloping valley before us, rushing toward our potential salvation, perhaps both figuratively and metaphorically. It was somewhat ironic that a church might be the place we feel the safest during a situation like this.

By the time we were back on the level, a steady trickle of rain had set in, the clouds overhead darkening to the point where they began to match the color of the Crag they sat against. It wasn't long before it transitioned fully to torrential curtains that pelted us with water and the occasional loose pine needle and tiny beads of ice. This was shaping up to be a powerful storm, and I begged that the structure we had seen from the valley was sound enough to withstand the onslaught that was rapidly approaching.

After several minutes of running as fast as the group could manage, trusting only the direction and instincts of Heather to lead us to safety, we came across long-since abandoned rail tracks, overgrown with weeds and shrubs, a canopy of tree branches creating a sort of tunnel that ran in either direction. Without a second thought, Heather brought the group to the right, following the length of the iron trail, the pellets of hail growing in size as we progressed, reaching the size of golf balls within moments. The trees overhead groaned as they stood against the wind, the branches clattering against each other.

Before we knew it, the tunnel gave way to a clearing filled with decaying wooden structures, many of which had already collapsed into heaps of lumber and overgrowth. The remnants of a crudely paved road formed alongside the tracks, lined with tall grasses and spindly brush. The rails veered off to the left, connecting with what might've once been a station of sorts had it not caved in the middle and slumped to its rear so that it looked as though it had been deflated. Following the stone road, we raced for the tallest structure that sat near the center of the settlement: a pine church.

It was perhaps only three stories tall at most, most of its height coming from the narrow tower that protruded from its front, topped with a spire that ascended above the treetops. All of its windows had been broken, with jagged pieces of glass still fixed in some of the frames. The whole building seemed completely uninviting with its haunting dominion over the town and pitch-black interior that could be gleaned through the empty windows. But we were in no position to be selective with the storm bearing down on us with growing strength every minute.

Heather tore the front door open, nearly ripping the soggy, rotten wood from the frame, beckoning us inside like a coach sending a high school football team to the field. Once we had all gathered in the entry hall, she slammed the door shut behind us, the iron latch engaging with an audible click. Fortunately, the interior was almost completely dry, the perhaps century of neglect having minimal impact on the roof. Chuck was the first to speak after we all had a moment to catch our breaths in the dark.

"Anyone got a flashlight on them?"

"I think the doc had one. Let me check..." responded Harvey, rummaging through the satchel of what remained of Harlan's articles. While he did so, I retrieved my lighter from my back pocket, tossing back the cover and giving it a flick. The dim, orange flame illuminated the immediate area around us, casting dancing shadows off of randomly strewn pieces of wooden furniture.

"That works, too," Chuck muttered. The group began to break apart, investigating the interior of the church. It was a singular room that was perhaps no more than fifteen feet by thirty, with a half dozen rows of pews, the musty smell of decaying paper and wood hung in the relatively still air. I could hear someone coughing, most likely one of the Washburn brothers. Satisfied that the church likely wouldn't collapse in on us while we slept, the group gathered near the back row of benches in the largest available space. Here, Harvey produced a small, battery-powered lantern from the cloth satchel and placed it on the floor so that it lit up the room. We gathered around it to rest for the first time since setting out earlier that morning—the group now completely drained.

"So what now?" Jakob asked no one in particular.

"I don't think that is going to matter until the morning at least," Heather responded, exhausted.

"Where do you think those tracks lead?" I asked. The other members of the group were silent for a moment as the realization dawned on them.

"Probably all the way back to society," Chuck responded, his cavalier attitude making a resurgence.

"There's no way of knowing that, guys. If this place was built a hundred or so years ago, who's to say that those go anywhere other than other ghost towns? I bet they'll connect up to something somewhere, but we'd run out of supplies long before then. We're down to two days of food, and that's if we really stretch it," Heather sighed.

"Well, now that the fat one is gone, we can probab—" Jakob started before being tackled by Marcus in a flurry of rage. It took both Harvey and Heather to remove the disheveled man from the arrogant man-child.

"Chuck, you need to get him under control before he gets himself, or the rest of us, killed," Heather yelled, pointing at the smirking Washburn, blood already streaming down from his nose. She turned, lowering her face so that it was inches from his. "Don't think I won't put you down and bury you outside this church," she threatened, her voice hauntingly cold. The smile disappeared from Jakob's face, the grim realization setting in that he had only made more enemies who wanted to see him in the dirt.

"Well, let's not do anything rash here," Chuck said, standing up and extending his hands.

"Right now, *your* brother is a threat to the survival of the rest of this group. I will do what is necessary if he continues attempting to sabotage us," she barked. Defeated, Chuck sat back down.

With the tension dissipating, exhaustion began to creep into the corners of our minds. We shared a few bites of loose granola and finished off the last of the drinking water. With the benefit of the rain, we placed our empty canteens outside so that they might fill up while the storm raged on overhead. While scoping out a spot for myself to rest for the night, I noticed Harvey sitting alone in one of the pews near the front of the church. I unrolled my sleeping bag to claim the back right corner and approached him.

"This seat taken?" I asked, sliding into his right. I noticed he was kneeling, his large hands folded as they rested against his legs. He snickered, shaking his head as a smile wrapped around his face.

"By all means..." he responded warmly.

"Didn't know you were religious," I remarked.

"I'm not really. But I won't claim to have all the answers either. I can be wrong. And, right now, I'm really hoping I am wrong," Harvey responded, a slight tremor in his voice. I sat next to him for a moment, listening to the sound of the wind and rain colliding against the church. I could hear him muttering something under his breath, perhaps a prayer of some sort, but I could not make it out.

"Do you think we're going to make it out of this?" I asked solemnly, the words just falling out of my mouth before I could think about it any longer. *I am exhausted*, I thought to myself, instantly regretting bringing the subject up. Harvey shifted uneasily in his seat, sliding back into the bench fully.

"Even if we do make it back, I don't know that we'll ever truly 'make it out.' These sorts of things can change a person forever. Right now, I just want to see my wife again, and I will hold on for as long as it takes to do that," he responded, oddly calm and collected, with a refinement that I had never heard out of him before.

"Me too."

He put a large hand on my shoulder and pulled me in. "You'll see her again someday, Sam. I'm sure of it."

"Hey guys—" a voice called out from behind, "found something everyone might want to see."

Without any further words, we both stood up and returned to the group to find Marcus knelt down next to the doctor's open satchel, something concealed in his hands.

"What did you find?" Heather asked, crouching next to him.

"It's a flare gun," he responded, revealing the heavy-gauge pistol painted in a vibrant yellow. On the floor next to him were three cylinders, likely the flares.

"Won't do us any good right now," Chuck stated, gesturing with open hands in the air. Conveniently, as if by command, a flash of lightning followed by a loud crack of thunder rang out around us, suddenly making the church feel small and unsafe.

"Of course not. But once this front clears..." Heather responded. She turned to Marcus. "Did any of the flares survive?"

"It's hard to tell. I could only find these three, but I feel like one of them has got to work at least."

"If the storm clears by morning, we should test it. I'm sure there are other people out there that will see it," Harvey added.

"Do you think anyone is looking for us?" I asked the group. Chuck shook his head, looking at the floor.

"Knowing Harlan for as long as I have, he has people on standby and aware of the hiking trip, but the itinerary had us out here for almost a week and a half. I don't think anyone is looking for us yet. Our best bet is another group also being out here and seeing the flare go off. But I doubt anyone is going to know where we are—this ghost town is probably not on any modern maps. We'd need to be near a notable geological feature..." he started before trailing off, evidently deep in thought. "We're going to have to climb the Crag."

# TEN

"You cannot be serious, Chuck," Heather protested. There were whispers amongst the other members of the group.

"I mean, we don't have to go all the way up, but it will be much easier to find us if the flare goes off from there as opposed to here—in the middle of nowhere," he countered. "Besides, whatever wild animal is coming after us is probably going to have a much harder time getting us up there."

"We don't have the equipment to even go up the Crag. This would be suicide," Marcus interjected feebly.

"It is suicide to stay down here. We either start starving to death, or that animal picks us off one by one. I'd rather take my chances with the Crag—at least that has the highest probability of maybe a few of us surviving this whole ordeal," the older Washburn hissed, profound contempt in his icy-cold tone. We all sat speechless for some time, listening to the wind howling outside, rocking the old frame of the church so that it felt as though we were aboard a ship, sailing in the blackness of night on rough waters.

"What about the train tracks?" Harvey asked, breaking the silence. Chuck scoffed at the suggestion as if the mere thought of it was beneath him.

"Heather is right; those probably don't go anywhere. Think about it—have you ever even seen tracks in Wendell or Ackerman? No? Do you want to take your chances on them?" he argued, his tone incredulous.

"Okay, that's enough. We really need to establish a plan we can all work with, even if we don't agree with it. Let's start with the rifle. When we run out of food, we can use it for hunting game. That would last us a little longer," Heather ordered, setting the rifle down in the middle of the crude circle we sat in.

"Every round we waste on food is one that could be used to stop whatever is following us," Jakob insisted. Perhaps, for the first time, he was right, and I hated that I agreed with him.

"How many rounds do you have then?" Heather returned, her eyes rolling subtly.

"I had twelve shots. So eleven after factoring in the one you wasted."

"Get those out for me," she barked. After letting out a forced sigh, Jakob retrieved his pack and rummaged through its contents. A few seconds went by, and his work became more erratic before finally beginning to remove whole items from the bag, tossing them indiscriminately to the ground. A moment later, the cloth pack lay, deflated and empty, on the wooden floor, Jakob's usually smug face completely stoic.

"Well?"

"I couldn't find the other clip."

"What do you mean? You lost it? How on earth did you manage that? You *cannot* be serious right now. I had such a low opinion of you, and yet, you somehow still find a way to go even lower," she spat, her words cutting into him like daggers. The younger Washburn said nothing and simply began putting his articles back into the pack.

Pressing her fingers against the bridge of her nose and closing her eyes, Heather said, "Okay. So we've got five shots remaining in the rifle. That's not a lot of room for error, nor is it a lot for getting game if we end up being here a while longer."

She paused, sighing, before continuing. "I think Chuck's plan is the best option we've got right now. That way, we can conserve our ammunition for defense, provided someone actually comes to rescue us."

"But the tracks—" I started to protest, feeling that everyone was failing to see the point, but Heather held up her hand to silence me.

"The only way we get through this is by working together. Don't make me carry you, bound, up the Crag."

Realizing that I had nowhere else to go and believing every word of her threat, I conceded defeat and held my tongue.

"So, are you military or what?" Chuck asked after a moment, leaning back, away from the blue light of the lantern so that his face was cast in shadow.

"Marine. Former," she responded concisely, signifying this was the end of the discussion for her. Yet, the older Washburn persisted.

"Well, that part is pretty obvious. The real question is— why here and now? You were so against leading the pack, yet you did it anyway," he pressed as if trying to conduct an interview for his radio station.

"Bad memories," she answered coldly.

"I hate to break it to you, but we've all got baggage here.

Harlan may not have expressly said that we were all his patients, but it's pretty apparent that he just plucked his favorite faces from therapy. I'd expect even a jarhead such as yourself to see that. So what's your story? It's not like we've got anything else to talk about anyway."

"I don't want to talk about it," she affirmed, her eyes lowering.

"Fine, I guess I'll go first then to get the crowd warmed up!" Chuck exclaimed, rubbing his hands together with an uncanny glee. He proceeded to tell us a story about how, when he was a teenager, he broke into the homestead liquor cabinet so that he could bring a fresh bottle of Kentucky bourbon to a friend's ranch a few miles down the road. On the way, he detailed how he was drinking from something else but stated that he had thought it was okay because he waited until late that night so nobody else would be on the road.

It turned out that his assessment had been wrong, running another car off the road, causing it to crash head-on into a tree. He said he never stopped to check, figuring someone else might happen upon them to help. The next morning, he found out that it had been his father in the other vehicle, the man dying of blood loss several hours after the accident with no one around to save him.

"Chuck... why on earth are you sharing this?" Heather asked, both confused and disgusted. We all turned to face him, equally puzzled by the shocking revelations he shared as though it were nothing more than a casual conversation between close friends.

"I... I've been seeing him a lot... My Pa. He's been in my dreams ever since we set foot out here. Besides, this is supposed to be therapeutic, after all. Why else would the doctor have brought us all the way out here if not to 'get in touch with ourselves' or something?" He seemed sincere in an odd way, a stark contrast to his usual front. "Jakob is the only other person that knew, well, besides Harlan."

"And I've never forgiven you for it," the younger Washburn muttered.

"Alright. Who's next?" Chuck asked, searching the faces of the group for the next victim before coming to a stop at Marcus. "String bean, what's your story?"

"I... uh... used to work in the medical industry. Specifically the terminal illness ward of a hospital over in Portland. We'd get these patients from time to time that were suffering. Like really bad. Off-the-charts pain where even the strongest doses of painkillers couldn't really do anything. Any more would probably have killed them. They'd beg me to 'put a little extra' in when I'd swap out their intravenous medications. Eventually, I cracked, pitying them... I put down three people that way before I couldn't do it anymore. The hospital opened investigations, but they were never able to pin it on me. I think they knew, though," Marcus shared, his voice quivering.

"I didn't peg you for an 'Angel of Death' there," Chuck responded. "Remind me never to go to whatever place you work now."

"I'm not in healthcare anymore. I restore bikes. Working with my hands to get my mind off them..." Marcus trailed off, his eyes glossing over. Chuck then turned to me, sizing me up.

"My wife died in a natural gas explosion because I left the stove on. The blaze also killed a firefighter," was all I was capable of conjuring up in my exhaustion. It was also a story I did not want to discuss anymore, especially with the likes of the Washburn brothers present.

"Well, that's pretty anti-climactic. Anyway, what about

you, Harvey? Got any tales for the group session? Going to be difficult to top," Chuck probed, smiling at him, seemingly amused with himself. Harvey proceeded to share the same story about the young deckhand that had been washed overboard while he was on duty, his deep voice cracking when he retold it, though he neglected to mention how he still called the boy's mother so many years later. By now, I could see the growing discomfort in the way the others sat, shifting uneasily from side to side in the flickering, blue wash of light cast by the electric lantern. The tension in the air was palpable.

"Well?" Chuck addressed Heather expectantly. She let out a long sigh, rubbing her face with one hand while she searched for a place to start from.

"Fine. I served in the Marines for three years, leading a squad of twelve other soldiers during the opening days of Desert Storm. We were part of the campaign to retake the Kuwait International Airport, supporting the First Marine Division. During the attack, we became separated from the primary fighting force. With enemy armor bearing down on us, I was caught between a rock and a hard place. I radioed in a mortar strike on our position and ordered my men to take cover in a nearby maintenance tunnel while I stayed in the ditch on the side of the road. I felt the Earth quake as that artillery rained down on us, and I thought I'd surely be dead after this. When the dust settled after five agonizing minutes of constant barrage, I checked on the others..." she paused, choking up. "A mortar had penetrated the access tunnel and detonated, killing all ten of my boys and mortally wounding the other two. One died screaming as I was pulling his top half out from under the rubble. The other, a sweet young man from Chicago—Chase—bled out in my arms. He was eighteen, fresh out of high school...

Enlisted to make his parents proud. And I had to ship what was left of him back to them in a plastic bag."

She wiped the tears from her eyes, flicking them away as she collected her composure. "But you know what was the worst part of it? I had to go tell their parents, all of them. Twenty-four people had their entire world come crashing down on them because of my order. The upper echelons told me that 'my order to hold the position' bought their armored units enough time to regroup and make a breakthrough, potentially saving dozens of lives—they called me a *hero* for doing what was 'necessary for the benefit of the campaign.' All I saw were twelve bodybags. I still see his face—Chase's—from time to time when I try to sleep. Do you want to know what his final words were, Chuck? Do you *really* want to know?"

Heather's agonized voice carried a twinge of rage hidden just below the surface as she goaded him on, taunting him for the corner he backed himself into. The older Washburn shifted uncomfortably, causing the floorboards beneath him to groan, his eyes fluttering from side to side as if looking for a way out. She breathed in deeply, summoning what little strength she hadn't yet spent that day.

"He looked me dead in the eyes and said: 'I don't want to die. Please save me. I don't want to die. I want my mom. Please.' Those damned words haunt every waking moment of my life, and I can never, *ever* forgive myself for the damage I did and the lives I ruined. It is only fair, in my mind, that I carry this weight until I die, too, and maybe then the thundering of those mortars will finally stop. So do you understand, now, why I don't want to be a leader? The only time I was ever trusted with the lives of others, I got them all killed," she finished, hanging her head low as she let the emotions she'd been wrestling with for so long take hold, sobbing quietly.

Marcus leaned over, wrapping his arms around her and pulling her in tightly, whispering words of comfort as she wept. I glanced over at Chuck, who looked as though he had seen a ghost, his complexion pale and eyes wide. *Serves him right for pressing that,* I thought to myself, disgusted. Though I knew that I had played a part in forcing her to take charge here and now, and I regretted having done that to her. I figured I would apologize in the morning once she had some time to rest and recover, letting those difficult memories fade back into the depths from where they came.

There was very little talk after that exchange, very likely the result of a combination of exhaustion and discomfort brought on. The whole conversation felt like a blur, almost as though it were impossible to prove it had really happened. I had learned a lot about the other members of the group who I now found myself sharing space with, their dark and twisted backgrounds altering my very perception of them in a way that I suddenly realized I never knew any of them before now. The memories that haunted me felt small by comparison.

As things began to wind down and the others took to their reclusive sleeping spots, I noticed the doctor's leather-bound journal protruding from a stack of supplies and snagged it before anyone else could notice—not that I thought they would stop me even if they had. I worked my way back through his meticulous entries, noting the dates as I progressed further—until the pages became barren. About a year into the past, the sheets of lined paper sat blank, sandwiched between expanses of lengthy text. Just three empty pages that signified what appeared to be a period of six months. I focused my attention on the last entry before the gap:

JULY 9TH, 1991

*WE LOST two shipments this past week alone to the DEA. I can feel them getting closer now, like dogs on the prowl. Peter told me the writing was on the wall and that we needed to turn ourselves in to get a lighter sentence. I had the twins take care of him. He might've been the rat we were looking for, but only time will tell. We are dissolving the enterprise for now and will regroup when they've backed off some more. We're all in over our heads.*

SKIPPING over the three empty pages, I read his next entry:

JANUARY 27TH, 1992

*THE FEDS FOUND where I put Peter and the twins. Dead men tell no tales. I think I am in the clear now. I left no loose ends. All of the remaining funds have been safely hidden in the stockpile, and I will retrieve those when I feel the time is right. I'd love to retire to someplace warm, and I can disappear. I'll have to do some research on Central America. For now, it is best that I stick to my day job treating these psychopaths and schizophrenics. I think it makes for a great cover if they ever do come knocking. No one is going to suspect a pillar of the community. One more trip, and I can make my grand escape.*

THE MORE I READ, the more I was disturbed by what I found. His journal elaborately described the massive criminal enterprise that he masterminded in our county, distributing narcotics. And I could not believe any of it. In the years that I had known him, the notion that he was a kingpin in a drug ring had never once crossed my mind, nor would I have guessed he was even remotely capable of murder. But perhaps that was the same situation we all faced here—not everyone is who they claim to be.

As I neared the end of his entries, I began to notice peculiarities. His writing tone shifted from a sense of arrogance to one that more closely resembled what a cornered animal might act like—a looming sense of dread and no way out. Eventually, and with what appeared to be great hesitation on his part, he began to divulge secrets that somehow felt of greater significance than homicide. The enigmatic text spoke of dreams—haunting perversions of reality where he faced down a shadowy, near-invisible enemy that lurked in the dark corners of his mind, taunting him. His depictions became more erratic, choosing words far beneath his level of intelligence. It felt less like he was documenting his life and more like he was talking to himself.

His final passages, dated during our hiking trip, described gruesome details of this creature—the same one that I had been seeing and perhaps the others too. Harlan had grown paranoid, but his hubris kept him from admitting that there was something far and beyond dangerous that was hunting him—hunting us. He knew he should've turned back but chose not to. He mentioned the stockpile again. *Perhaps the funds were out here somewhere, and he intended to collect now. Was that why he didn't want to turn back?* I wondered. It wouldn't matter much because he did not detail where it was or how to find it, whatever it ultimately was. And it wouldn't do us any good anyway. *Dead men tell no tales.*

---

THE STORM CONTINUED RAGING on outside our meek shelter, the aged, wooden walls groaning as they bore the brunt of the wind bashing against them. The others had since laid down for the night, relenting to the exhaustion. Fighting the urge to sleep, I joined Harvey back in his pew, sitting silently in the growing dark as the battery-powered lantern waned. Occasionally, the interior would erupt into light with the split-second crack of lightning, only to be plunged deeper into darkness afterward.

"I read through the doctor's journal," I blurted out sometime after sitting down, not entirely sure why I felt the need to share. Harvey turned to face me, perplexed.

"Not to be rude, but doesn't that feel wrong at all? For all intents and purposes, the man is dead, and you read through his personal belongings," he scolded. I agreed that this was probably a morally wrong thing to do at best, but it was ultimately a necessity.

"He was having the dreams, too. For months," I added, deciding that I wouldn't share what else I had found. *Perhaps it is best that he be remembered by how we all saw him and not by his actions or what he truly thought of us.* Harvey's face twisted in confusion, tossing his hands up.

"I know you all have been talking about having these 'dreams,' and it seems to be happening to everyone now, but

I still don't know what you are talking about. Why is it that I'm the only one not seeing this thing or having these nightmares?" he asked, sounding frustrated. I shrugged as I truly did not know. *What was different about him?*

"I'm not sure it matters much if it's coming for all of us."

"But what *is* it?" He was asking questions that I also wished I had the answers for, but they always remained just out of reach—hiding in the dark.

"Whatever it is, I just hope that we lost it," I said aimlessly.

"If it is really an animal, I think it is going to have a hard time tracking us through this. We put a lot of distance between us and that camp, and this weather should wash away our trail pretty good," Harvey consoled, perhaps trying to convince himself of it too. Just as I thought that I could relax, I heard the church door creak open. We both whipped around on the bench to see Marcus' frail frame against the torrents of rain outside—the rifle clutched in one hand, the lantern hanging in the other. He was staring at the both of us, his eyes wide.

Immediately, we bolted for him as we knew what he was going to do. Much to our dismay, he turned around and galloped into the storm, far faster than either of us would've expected him capable of. However, despite his head start and a several-yard lead on us, he slipped on the wet cobblestones in the road, toppling to the ground and giving us the time to catch up.

"What the hell do you think you are doing?!" Harvey boomed, his voice nearly drowned out by the downpour all around us. He took Marcus by the shoulders, shaking him like a doll. But he did not respond, his mouth was agape, and his eyes remained fixated on something far beyond. Then, without warning, he tore away violently with a strength we didn't anticipate—bashing Harvey in the chest with the rifle, who toppled to the side, the air knocked out of him.

Attempting to grab hold of Marcus myself, he brought the barrel of the gun up to my face, the dark hole inches away from my nose. I noticed it in his eyes—a pure, rabid rage. I felt it in my stomach that he was going to shoot me where I stood, but he didn't.

"I can't let it get me!" he shouted, backing away from me slowly.

"You are safer with us, Marcus. You know that! Put the gun down and come back with us," I pleaded, trying to defuse the situation. By now, Harvey was back on his feet and standing at my side. I didn't know what to do next and felt completely at the mercy of a man—a wild animal—backed into a corner.

But something caught my attention out of the corner of my eye. In the distance, I felt as though I had seen movement by the dilapidated station. Suddenly, there was a flash of lightning that illuminated the whole clearing and the remains of the town. To my horror—standing at the entrance of the overgrown tunnel of pine that engulfed the train tracks—was the creature, its skeletal body glistening and maw of a mouth hanging open. I could've sworn it was almost smiling at us.

I glanced up at Harvey, who was now a pale white and rigid in his stance. *He saw it, too.* In the commotion, Marcus had backed away from us even further, his back to it. *He has no idea it's out there, waiting for him.*

"Marcus! It's right there!" I cried as he turned around and started running for the tracks. Another flash of lightning. The creature was nowhere to be seen now. We watched as Marcus—and the dying lantern—were swallowed whole by the hungry darkness. We both stood in silence as we were pelted by the rain, unsure of if we should pursue him or not. I began to doubt if I had truly seen anything or if the extreme levels of sleep deprivation I was experiencing had finally caught up to me. Moments later, from somewhere in the vast expanse beyond, I could've sworn I had heard screaming.

# ELEVEN

"Marcus!" we called out in unison, our voices drowned out by the thundering rain that pounded the earth around us. It was almost as though we were completely alone—raging against something like the vastness of the ocean. By now, the others had heard us and were rushing out into the storm, stopping just at our sides, not daring to go any further forward, a mix of confusion and bewilderment plastered their faces.

"What the hell is going on? Where is Marcus?" Heather shouted, shielding her eyes from the rain with her arm.

"He ran out there with the gun and the lantern—" I started before Jakob pushed past me, heading straight for the tracks where I had last seen the creature.

"Get back here!" Chuck commanded, trying to force down the dread that crept up into his voice.

"Our only defense is out there! He couldn't have gotten far," he whined. By now, his older brother had him by the shoulders, shaking him—reminding me of how Harvey had just done the same a few minutes prior.

"Forget the gun, damn it! I already lost Pa. I ain't losing you too." His mustache and beard appeared ragged, a combination of being soaked and the days of neglect without having his grooming kit.

"I saw it," I yelled. "It was waiting for him. I don't think there is anything we can do now."

A quick glance over at Heather led me to believe she was silently crying, but the rain pouring down her face made it difficult to tell. I placed a hand on her shoulder. "I'm sorry. We did what we could."

She fell into me with dead weight, all of her strength failing as she heaved. I couldn't even imagine what she might be feeling at that moment—to have bared all of that inner turmoil only to lose both of your close friends within twenty-four hours of each other, all while stranded in the middle of nowhere with an unknown entity stalking your every move. I did my best to support her while she wept, but the growing unease of knowing it was out there and we were standing in the open made me push to return to the relative safety the church provided.

*It was real. Not just a figment of my imagination—it was actually, really... real.* I didn't know what to make of this revelation, and I couldn't decide if this made me feel any better or worse as a result. *It can't be. Surely, that was just your eyes and ears playing tricks on you. Marcus is probably a mile away now. Might make it somewhere for help by the time the sun comes up in the morning. You don't know that Harvey saw it, either.* I turned to face the behemoth of a man. *I need to talk to him.*

"I think we should head back inside. It's not safe out here," I thought aloud. The others agreed, and we returned to the confines of the church, feeling even more alone now than before—as if all the warmth we previously had was extinguished. If Harvey hadn't been so out of it, he probably would've made a joke about having no wind in our sails or something along those lines. Instead, he sheepishly returned to his spot in the pew. Even though I wanted nothing more than to leave him to his business, I needed to know if he saw it, too.

"Did you see what I saw?" I asked, sliding in next to him. He nodded, not saying a word nor lifting his lowered head to look at me. This man had been so full of life and character when I met him, and all of it was seemingly gone. I wondered if he would ever be able to recover from this series of events should we make it out alive. As I stood up, his hand shot out, grasping tightly around my forearm, gently pulling me back down as if begging for me to stay. And so I did.

We sat in silence for hours, but it felt like days. At some point, I noticed Harvey dozed off, snoring loudly as he slouched over the bench in front of us. Despite being generally uncomfortable and longing for any semblance of luxury my sleeping bag might've provided in comparison, I did not want to abandon him in his time of need. He had been there for me when I needed it. Eventually, the storm began to let up, and I could not fight off the exhaustion I had been resisting for so long.

---

I KNEW I would dream tonight—there was no point in fighting it anymore. But, much to my surprise, I did not find myself immediately swarmed by the creature, nor did I feel its all too familiar presence. Instead, I was standing at the edge of Ackerman at twilight, the air cool with the sun just below the horizon. The sky was a pale but serene mixture of blue, purple, and yellow. At first, I felt at ease—until I noticed that I was still alone.

I dared not to move for some time, wondering what might happen when the last light of day gasped and died, but it never came. The world hung in a constant, unending state of twilight. Realizing that nothing was happening, I began to walk into town, following the worn-down concrete of the sidewalk. The further I went, the more uncomfortable I felt. *There are no cars here either,* I thought to myself. Not seeing other people made sense since they were fairly rare in my dreams, but not seeing any signs of other people? That felt wrong.

I eventually lost track of the time and how long I had been there. It was difficult to grasp when my watch stopped working and the state of limbo somewhere between day and night. I had the opportunity to explore buildings I had never been to before, whose interiors were all the same. *Figures. I've never been to these places, of course, I don't know what they look like inside.* Eventually, I found myself standing at the entrance to Harvey's Diner; the glass door fogged over, so I could not make out the inside. But I could hear the haunting sound of a jukebox playing songs from a bygone era somewhere within. Perhaps against my better judgment, I entered the building, the bell on the door chiming as I did so.

Much like the rest of Ackerman, the interior was completely devoid of all signs of life. The fluorescent bulbs flickered overhead, washing the room in an eerie, borderline sterile light. I noted the lonesome jukebox sitting across from me on the far wall, providing entertainment to nobody, its lights providing the only sense of warmth I had experienced since arriving here. Without much thought, I drew closer to it—like a moth to a flame.

"So what'll it be, Sam?" a familiar voice boomed to my right, startling me. I whirled around to see Harvey standing behind the counter, his writing pad and pen in hand, a smile stretching from ear to ear on his face. Unsure of what I should do, I cautiously approached, taking a seat on one of the stools in front of him.

"Harvey?" I asked hesitantly.

"That's the name! Now, we've got a great breakfast special on today. Bacon and eggs, just how you like them. Can I put you down for that?"

The more he spoke, the more I felt unsettled. *This feels almost wrong now.* It was like a real-life caricature of the man I had just spent the past few days watching break down completely until there was almost nothing left.

"This isn't real. You're not Harvey." I stood up, feeling disgusted, and began for the door.

"Of course I am! Well, at least from before you came along…" His words sounded cheerful, but the delivery was seeped in hatred. I slowly turned around, feeling as though I had just been punched in the gut. "What? Did you think I was just like you? Some tortured soul that you just had to bring down to your level because you can't stand seeing other people happy? Or maybe you were just jealous of the life I had before you got us all killed?" He was still smiling—an uncanny, toothy grin.

"No! None of that is true," I responded, trying to defend myself against the onslaught. But his words cut deep, and I began to doubt my own intentions. *Had I really done this to him?*

"Sam, Sam. Poor Sam. I need everyone to pity me,

Sam," he mocked. "You got me and everyone else killed. It is all your fault."

By now, the jukebox had begun to falter, the old-timey music cracking and popping as if gasping for air. The flicker of the lights above grew more apparent.

"I didn't get anyone killed. This isn't my fault. You were the one who wanted me to go on that damned hike anyway!" I cried, fighting back the tears that were welling up at the corners of my eyes. Harvey was no longer smiling.

"You brought it with you, Sam. You know you did."

"Harlan was seeing it long before I did. If anything, it was his fault for this mess!"

The pleading felt useless—I knew I didn't believe my own words, even if they felt true when I spoke them. I could hear my heart thumping in my chest. The jukebox had stopped completely. I looked around, feeling *its* presence again—the chill of the air mixing with a new smell: the sickly sweet stench of decay.

I whirled back around to face Harvey, crying, "I am sorry. I am sorry that I did all of this. What more do you want from me? What more can I possibly give to make any of this right?"

He did not respond immediately, but began smiling once more.

"Sam. Life isn't some kind of transaction you can thoughtlessly make. Your debts can never be repaid..." He paused, cocking his head to one side, "...but I do appreciate the effort. For what it's worth, I considered you one of my closest friends, even in the short time we knew each other."

I watched as the fading light of twilight turned to the black of night through the frosted windows out of the corner of my eye. I raced for the door, pressing hard against its surface, but it would not give no matter how fiercely I pushed—almost as though I were trying to move a wall of stone. Harvey let out a chuckle that seemed to echo deep into my head.

"What's going on? Why can't I open the door?" I asked, trying to keep my rapidly evaporating cool.

"Why don't you stay a while, Sam? Come, kick up your boots, and relax while you still can. By the looks of things, it won't be too long now."

Behind me, the door rattled in its frame, a looming shadow just beyond its hazy surface. The stench of decay grew stronger, and I could hear deep breathing emanating from behind the glass, the sound of which sent shivers down my spine. I did my best to fight the panic that was setting in. *I was trapped in here. The wolf is at the door, and I have nowhere to go—nowhere to hide.*

Realizing that I didn't have much else I could do in this terrible situation, I returned to my stool in front of Harvey, a fresh plate of eggs and bacon steaming on the counter. I didn't notice when it had appeared, just that it hadn't been there when I made for the exit. But it smelled delicious, and I was suddenly overcome with a hunger greater than I had ever experienced before. Harvey set a hot cup of coffee down next to my plate, the polished ceramic surface reflecting the room almost as though it were a perfect mirror.

As I finished my meal, I noticed the faint sound of the jukebox playing a tune I hadn't heard in many years—the same song that played during the first dance with my wife. It seemed to grow louder the more I focused in on it, the flicker of the overhead lights seeming to relax. Where I expected to find sadness and regret, I instead found a bittersweet sense of tranquility and appreciation. I missed her deeply, perhaps more in this moment than all others combined.

"Beautiful song, Sam. It was a good choice," Harvey expressed in his characteristically friendly tone, the same one that had been missing since I entered the diner. I let out a deep sigh, my eyes watering up. "You miss her, don't you?"

"I would sacrifice the rest of my life if it meant I could share this dance with her one more time—just one more minute."

Harvey nodded, picking up my empty plate and coffee mug, returning them to the kitchen—leaving me alone in the main room, the song washing over me. I listened as it flourished, the strings and piano melding together as they played in harmony—I knew it was coming to its conclusion. When Harvey reappeared a moment later, he slid something across the empty counter toward me. Upon further examination, I realized it was my lighter that I kept in my back pocket at all times.

"She gave this to you, didn't she?"

"Yes. I never really knew the meaning, but I never went anywhere without it. She always said it would keep me safe," I responded, vividly recalling the memory of her handing me the lighter wrapped in loose cloth as we left the wedding reception. I remembered how happy I was in that moment. The song was reaching its ending now—only the lonely piano remained as all other instruments of the ensemble faded away like a distant memory. The haunting finality of the end approached with its arms outstretched like an embrace with someone loved but lost somewhere along the way.

"Time's almost up now," Harvey said, polishing a mug in his hand with a dish rag.

"What's going to happen next?" I asked, growing tense.

I could hear it pacing back and forth outside, its claws scraping against the concrete. Harvey just shook his head and smiled.

"Nobody knows. Isn't that the best part of it?"

"Quit talking like that, and just tell me what that is out there," I begged as I pointed at the door. He set the mug he was polishing down on the counter and leaned forward.

"I think you already know exactly what it is. But like everyone else, you don't want to accept it until it's too late," he whispered. As he pulled away, the jukebox crackled and fell silent once more, taking with it what little life was left in the room. The fluorescent lights overhead dimmed, flickering every few seconds in a pattern like waves—all emanating from the entrance. Harvey began humming the tune the jukebox had been playing for the last few minutes.

"Harvey... please," I pleaded, not knowing exactly what I needed from him.

"You have the lighter, right?" he asked. I reached down and plucked it from my pocket, where I had returned it to moments ago. "Good. Keep it close. You are going to need it."

"What do you mean—" I started before the room suddenly plunged into total darkness, Harvey disappearing without a trace. The space immediately filled with the smell of decay as the front door fell from its hinges, the glass shattering across the checkered, linoleum floor and scattering like insects. The thing crept in slowly at first, its gangly arms wrapping around the door frame as it pulled its gaunt figure through the opening. I couldn't make out any of its features in the darkness as only its silhouette was visible—the pale moonlight beyond barely enough to show its outline.

It let out a dissonant roar that made my eardrums throb in pain, shattering the glass windows to either side of it. The next few seconds seemed to slow down as it lunged toward me, closing the gap of a couple of yards as though it were nothing. With very little time to react, I ignited the lighter still held tightly in my hand. To my surprise, the creature recoiled and lost its balance, colliding sharply with my shoulder, sending us both crashing onto the floor—my lighter sent careening into a booth. As if it had been doused in gasoline, the seat burst into a tower of flames that spread quickly. Before I even had a chance to stand back up, half of the room had been engulfed in a roaring fire.

Without any further thought, I barreled for the exit—not daring a glimpse over my shoulder to see if it was pursuing me. It wasn't until I was back on the empty street that I realized my lighter was gone, one of the last tokens from my previous life, destroyed in the raging blaze that consumed the diner. It—and, to another extent, Maria—had saved my life. I felt no greater urge than to go back in and brave the scorch to try and retrieve it, its loss feeling as though it were on par with the loss of a close friend.

Instead, I collapsed on the street, crying hard into the wet pavement as a thick fog rolled in. Within minutes, I was engulfed in the cloud, the only sign of the fire being the crackling heat and the faint, orange glow that penetrated the mist. From somewhere in the beyond, the sound of jazz began to play—its notes heavily compressed and somewhat distorted as if it were emanating from a cheap stereo system —like a car. Upon hearing it, I sat up and looked around. I couldn't discern the direction it was coming from—it felt like it was everywhere all at once—surrounding me like some kind of ghostly entity.

Feeling a sense of foreboding, I climbed to my feet and attempted to reorient myself, but my sense of direction had failed in the viscous fog. I could no longer see nor hear the fire that had destroyed the diner only moments prior. The world nearby seemed to shift as though I were being transported on a flying disc—the cloud swirling around me. And as if blown away by a large fan, it dissipated in an instant, revealing that I was no longer in the middle of Ackerman. I was now standing on the street before the vacation home once more, its burnt-out windows gaping at me with their haunting blackness within. However, the sound of jazz continued to play from some indiscernible location, its oddly comforting melody soothing my nerves.

While gazing up at the scorched structure, I noticed movement in one of the windows. It was incredibly subtle, and I was initially convinced that it had been nothing more than a curtain fluttering in the breeze. Except the air was deadly still. As I attempted to focus more, I felt my eyes strain as though what I was trying to make out was burning my retinas as I did so. When I stopped to rub them to ease the pain away, the movement was gone. Feeling a sudden sense of fear, thinking that it was the creature and that it was coming, I frantically turned around, searching for a place to run to. But the jazz music was still playing. *This has never happened before,* I thought to myself while trying to calm down. *It's always quiet when it comes for me.*

I paused for a moment, attempting to digest the thoughts racing through my head. *Had I killed it back at the diner?* I had no idea if that was possible or if it even made any sense, but I felt an odd sensation of relief. I almost knew that it was not here with me—the feeling it gave when it was near was almost indescribable up until now, when I didn't feel it at all. With nothing else to do, I sat back down in the middle of the road below a humming streetlight and listened to the melody play out in the crisp air around me.

I stirred, what felt like mere moments later, to the warmth of the rising sun shining on my face. The storm had passed sometime in the night and gave way to clear skies. Beyond the confines of the worn-down church, the sweet sound of birdsong filled the air. In a way, it mimicked some of what I had been listening to in my dream, and I wondered how much of that was just a subconscious influence at play. It wasn't until a moment later that the haunting memories of what had transpired last night returned. As I came to my senses further, I realized I had slumped over to my side and had been leaning against Harvey while I slept.

"That could not have been comfortable," he said when he noticed I was awake, smiling lightly.

"I think with how tired I was, anything would've done the trick. Honestly, I'm still very tired," I responded as I shifted and pulled away, stretching as I did so. There was an ungodly, painful twist in my neck that I tried to massage out, but it persisted nonetheless. "How long have you been up?"

"Since before sunrise, so probably an hour or two. I don't really know. I couldn't make out your watch and didn't want to wake you up," he answered. Feeling embarrassed, I let out an awkward chuckle, which he reciprocated. "You snore, by the way."

"So do you. I'm honestly surprised I even fell asleep," I returned as lightheartedly as I could manage, given the gravity of the situation we still found ourselves in. I glanced around the single room, searching the shadows for the others, but could not make them out. "Where is everyone else?"

"They went looking for Marcus as soon as first light. Heather is really torn up about it and wanted to go out alone, but Chuck wouldn't allow it unless he and his brother went with her. I think they mostly wanted to get the gun back, but I sure was surprised by it regardless," Harvey stated.

"I don't think they are going to find him," I muttered, recalling the last time I saw him as he disappeared into the darkness. Harvey shook his head as well.

"With the storm, I don't think they'd even have a chance of finding a trail to follow. And, that thing..."

*So he definitely saw it then,* I thought.

"I'm glad I wasn't the only one to see it. I feel like I've just been going crazy since the first time I saw it—"

"Wait, you've *seen* it in real life before?" interrupted Harvey, looking distraught.

"Remember that cave that Jakob wanted to go into when we first lost the doctor? I saw it there. The crazy thing is, I thought it was talking to me."

Harvey shook his head, rubbing the palms of his great hands into his eye sockets and taking shallow breaths through his open mouth, incoherently mumbling to himself.

"What the hell is happening to us? Are we going insane out here?" he asked though I assumed it probably wasn't for me to answer.

"I didn't say anything because I thought you'd think I was actually insane," I added. He began pacing back and forth in the aisle between the rows of benches, the old floorboards creaking beneath his weight. It appeared as though he hadn't really processed anything that had happened the past few days, and it was all crashing into him at once, the onset of nerves spilling over into full-blown panic before my eyes.

"Oh, god, we are actually going to die out here," I heard him mutter to himself between the frightened heaves for air. Before I had a chance to even try and calm the poor man down, the wooden door at the entrance to the church flew open, rattling the structure to the point where I was sure it might collapse in on itself, the other three members of the group piling in on top of each other in a mass of arms and legs frantically clambering. Their faces were all painted white with fear. They slammed the door behind them, Heather immediately motioning for Chuck to help her move the nearest bench in front of it while Jakob braced it to keep it from opening again.

"What is going on?" I called out, my heart already pounding. Nobody responded until the bench was firmly wedged against the door.

"There's no time! Get what you can carry. We've got to get out of here, now!" Heather ordered as she raced for her pack and supplies, the Washburn brothers doing the same. Within seconds, the door began to shake violently in its frame, the rusting hinges rattling like a snake. With no additional words, I vaulted over the back of the bench and crawled to my pack, stuffing what little I had removed from it back in. As I started rolling my sleeping bag, Heather tugged on my jacket collar and shouted, "Leave it!"

I did not protest as I tossed it aside—there was too little time to process what was going on, and the moment necessitated quick actions. As I stood back up, I watched as the others seemed to disappear in blurring streaks through an open door in the far, back left corner of the main room. Following Heather, we raced for the exit, not daring to look over our shoulders. I listened as the entryway door was torn from its frame, the ancient and brittle wood exploding in a shower of splinters, the pursuant letting out a wail that can only be described as blood-curdling and human-adjacent.

Back in the forest, we rushed as a loose pack of scared animals, all honing in on the Crag that was somewhere before us in the thicket. The vegetation around us blurred as we sprinted, and the world almost seemed to slow for a moment. I did not know if whatever was following the others was still after them or what it was, but I think I knew deep down and perhaps just didn't want to admit it. *It had us cornered. It was coming in for the kill.*

"Alright, stop!" Heather barked after a moment, glancing over her shoulder. The group hesitated, casting looks between each other and scanning our surroundings.

"It's still out there!" Chuck protested, gesturing forcefully in the direction we had just come. Jakob had hunched over, dry heaving and gasping for air.

"No, listen," she returned, quieter this time. The group paused and fell silent, the sounds of the forest bathing us in a sense of odd serenity. *How did she know about that?* I wondered to myself. There was definitely more to Heather and what she knew about this thing than she was letting on.

"I don't get it," Chuck huffed, crossing his arms. Heather approached him and placed the flare gun she had been carrying against his chest.

"If you can hear anything other than your own heartbeat, you're safe. Well, as safe as you can get, I guess."

"What the hell happened back there?" I demanded as I stepped forward, feeling a slight twinge of anger well up in my chest.

"We thought we found Marcus..." she started before trailing off, her gaze falling to the side.

"We were about a mile up the tracks. Started hearing him call our names, so we followed his voice. Led us to a clearing a couple hundred feet off to the side. In the near-perfect center was the rifle and the lantern. Jakob almost went for it before we noticed... damn thing was on top of us before we knew it. Like it was setting a trap," Chuck finished solemnly. I felt my heart sink at the last sentence.

"I thought you guys were just seeing it in your dreams? What the hell is it doing out here?" Jakob asked, his voice cracking as he was still trying to recover from the sprint. I exchanged glances with Heather and Chuck, both of whom looked deeply troubled.

"What now?" I queried, turning to face Heather.

"We stick to the plan from last night. We climb the Crag and signal for help with the flare gun," she responded, cold and calculating.

"And what happens if nobody comes?"

She did not answer, instead choosing to begin the trek toward the looming, gray pillar that just barely broke through the treetops.

---

We were much closer to the Crag than I thought we had been previously. The group had progressed without a single further word shared for another hour or so, judging by the progress of the sun in the sky—but it felt like an eternity on its own. At the end of our journey, we gathered near a rocky overhang at what I assumed was the start of the incline. Heather was examining the surface, even attempting to climb it at one point, before sliding back down.

"It's no good. Even with the proper equipment, the rocks will be too wet from the storm last night to climb.

We're going to have to wait for it to dry out," she muttered after joining us again.

"How long would that take?" Chuck asked, his tone a mixture of frustration and masked panic. Heather shrugged, looking up through the trees at the giant.

"If we get any amount of sun today, we might be able to this evening. But those clouds coming in are giving me concerns about that actually happening. I think we are going to have to make camp."

At this, I could feel the unease in the others as they began to shift in their stances nervously.

"We're out in the open. We'd be sitting ducks!" Jakob protested. He was right, though I hated to admit it. Shortly after, the remaining members of the group erupted into an argument with a cacophony of angry voices.

"I need all of you to shut up and listen to me!" Heather commanded, her demands breaking through the sound of chaos we were drowning ourselves in. "If we try to climb right now, I can all but guarantee that we will die. This is not a kiddie hill that your parents told you was a mountain when you were little to make you think you were some big shot for climbing it. This is a real, honest-to-God mountain with sheer cliffs and hundred-foot drops. The Crag has a body count in the dozens, and that is only counting those since the park service started keeping track in the Fifties. Trying to make that ascent, even with the proper gear and the right conditions, is a challenge. We have neither of those advantages right now. Honestly, we are talking about the difference between almost suicide staying down here and definite suicide!"

Nobody spoke or protested what she had shared, recognizing her authority and experience. I gave a quick look up through the branches of the great pines that surrounded us, taking in the dark and ominous shape of the Crag that reached for the heavens above it as if it were going to stab it. We were so close to a semblance of safety yet so far at the same time. It began to sink in that we all might die here at the foot of the mountain before ever having a chance at salvation. Then, an idea dawned on me.

"What if we fired off the flare from down here? I mean, we are close enough to it at this point that surely anyone looking will know it's by the Crag," I said with great enthusiasm. My hopes were quickly dashed when Heather shook her head.

"We've only got those three shots. And with the canopy of branches above us, you have a greater chance of starting a forest fire than getting one of those above them."

Chuck, stepping forward and waving the flare gun around in his hand, said, "Sam's got a point. I think we should try it." He glanced over at me and signaled his approval with the ever-so-subtle upward tilt of his chin and the faintest of smiles, his eyes glinting. Harvey also expressed his agreement.

"Alright, alright. Fine—waste the shots for all I care," she conceded, reaching into her pack and rummaging around for the three flares. Heather placed them into Chuck's hungry and eager hands, which quickly went to work loading the first slug into the chamber. With a brief "Here goes nothing," he fired it off. To our dismay, the round burst from the end of the barrel but did not ignite, disappearing somewhere above in the sky.

"Must've gotten wet or something," Jakob said aloud, though it likely made more sense that he was talking to himself than anyone in particular. His older brother placed the second charge into the gun after examining its exterior. I could see the growing anxiousness on his face as he pointed it at the sky again, pulling the trigger once more. This time, the round fired from the barrel with a violent whistle before igniting into a blinding red light. It soared up into the canopy of pine branches, nearly breaking through the barrier, but became caught. Within a few more seconds, it fizzled out in the damp pine needles that cradled it. Chuck went to load the last round, his hands shaking, but Harvey reached over and took the gun from him.

"Hey—" Chuck began to protest, attempting to take back what he believed belonged to him, but Harvey simply held it above his head as though the Washburn were a small child. If it weren't for the precarious situation we all found ourselves in, I would've found it incredibly amusing.

"You just wasted two shots. That's it. I'm not going to let your hubris get me killed," he boomed, causing Chuck to jump back, startled. Harvey returned the gun to Heather, who immediately tucked it into her belt for safekeeping after removing the final flare, smiling gently at him as he backed away. At that moment, it dawned on me just how much older she looked now compared to just a few days ago when we had met. The dark circles under her eyes and the deepening lines on her face made me wonder if perhaps I had started to look the same. If we survived this, I knew I would be fighting these haunting memories for the rest of my life.

---

After the tensions had subsided, we made camp at the base of the mountain, finding a relatively level area a few hundred feet away from where we had tried the flare gun an hour or so prior. With most of our supplies left behind in the church when we were attacked, nobody had their tents, and only Harvey had a sleeping bag at this point, which he volunteered to Heather, for which she thanked him but ultimately declined.

It was determined that night we would all take shifts to keep a lookout in case the creature was spotted. We knew it would be out there, circling us in the dark. Although I knew deep down that it wouldn't have mattered if someone was taking guard or not, it would get all of us if it really wanted to. But I couldn't shake the odd feeling I had about all of it. *If it was so quick and lethal, why take us out one by one? Was it playing with us?* I shuddered at the concerning thought.

As the sun set and the rolling hills and valleys nestled between them grew dark, cast in long shadows, we set up a small fire from what little dry wood we could scavenge in the area around us. The wood popped and hissed as the pine resin within burned, dripping into the dirt below like molasses. There was no banter tonight—nobody had the energy for it, regardless of the looming dread of impending danger. Attempting to break up the deafening silence around us, I poignantly asked Heather, "When are you going to tell us what you know about this thing?"

The group first looked at me and then turned to face Heather, who was now sitting up straight and shifting nervously, causing the shadows on her face to dance wildly. It was the confirmation I had been looking for. *I knew it.* After a moment of deep thought, opening and closing her mouth as if trying to find the words to start with, she took in a deep breath and let it out in a long and depressing sigh.

"It may come as a surprise to all of you, but my mother's side of the family has a long line of Native blood that can be traced back to the tribes in this region."

She paused to shake her head and breathe in again,

seemingly fighting some kind of internal battle with herself. "My ancestors lived on these lands, hunting, and fishing for centuries before the white men from the East began to settle. There is some truth to the story Chuck had shared that first night. There was a forgotten group that got caught in our lands during one of the fiercest winters our people had known. When their supplies ran out, they sent some of their strongest to us, begging for food. The Chief took pity on them and sent some of our own dwindling rations back with them. They never saw them again. It wasn't until the thaw that our hunters found the cave they held up in for all those months. The stripped bones of seventeen men, women, and children strewn about the space. The only intact body was that of a man who died from exposure, a half-eaten arm still clenched in his hands."

Heather lowered her head, running her hands through her black hair. There were some murmurs from the Washburn brothers as they exchanged their thoughts, concern, and discomfort in their eyes as they watched her from across the fire. I cast a quick glance over at Harvey, who was stoic as ever, his face empty.

"As was tradition, my ancestors buried them all and held ceremonies to dispel any 'evil spirits' that could've manifested from such wicked actions. Many said that they failed, and the tribes soon abandoned their homes, saying that the land was now tainted by a darkness that no man could ever undo. It was said that those who committed heinous actions against others would soon be driven to madness and, eventually, death itself," she finished, her voice tired as if strained by the weight of the story she had just shared.

"Why did you come back after you saw it that first time years ago?" I asked, perplexed.

"Climbing the Crag was previously seen as a writ of passage into adulthood for them. Maybe it was foolish, but I had wanted to do the same, to feel some connection to something far older than me. I did not believe the stories. How could anyone believe such things now?" she responded coldly.

"So it's some kind of—what—demon?" Chuck questioned, to which Heather just shrugged.

"That's all I know. My mother did not share much. Said it was bad to provoke such an evil entity."

"And it's after us because we've killed other people," I said to her, not sure if it was a question or a statement. To my dismay, she simply nodded.

"If there is even a shred of truth to the stories, then yes."

"Why is it coming after us now? I've gone on hikes with Harlan for years, and there was never a sign of some shadowy demon thing," Chuck stressed, his voice cracking though he tried to hide his apparent fear.

"Chuck... this is the first one where we've crossed the river. These are their lands... *its* hunting grounds," she responded. There was a moment of uncomfortable silence between anyone speaking, the sounds of the pine trees rustling in the light, evening breeze being the only thing keeping me sane in this pause.

"Until last night, I had never seen it. Not even in my dreams like the rest of you. What does that mean?" Harvey chimed in. It was actually a really good question and something I hadn't realized about him yet. We all turned expectantly to Heather, who shrugged, her eyes gazing off into the dark somewhere beyond.

"I'm sorry, Harvey. I really don't know."

"I... uh... I saw it before we came here," I said with extreme hesitation, knowing this might be more than the others could handle at the time. Heather turned toward me; her features lost in the flicker of the shadows cast on her face by the fire, her lips pressed firmly against each other in a grim frown.

"Sam. You need to forgive yourself," she said in a tone seemingly completely out of character for her, a soft and warm one unlike anything she had done before. The world seemed to melt away around us for a second, the shadowy silhouettes of the trees blurring into the background.

"What do you mean?" I asked, perplexed by the sudden change in her previously gruff and generally uncaring demeanor. She shook her head.

"The dead don't forgive."

The words seemed to echo around me, ringing in my ears like speakers turned all the way up. Despite hearing it before, I still didn't understand what it meant. I hunched forward, clasping my hands to the sides of my head, trying, in vain, to block the painful reverberations from entering, but it was no use—they were deeply burrowed into my skull. After several agonizing moments, it began to subside, disappearing into the depths of my consciousness. Sitting back up, I realized that the once lively fire was no more than smoldering embers, lightly flickering against the blackness that cloaked our surroundings.

"Sam?" I heard Heather whisper from somewhere beyond, though I could not make her out.

"Yeah?" I responded, wondering what was going on. *Did any of that just happen?* There was some light shuffling as she emerged from the darkness a few feet away, wrapped in a blanket. She sat down gently next to me but did not make eye contact.

"I'm glad you are up. My shift was coming to an end, and you're up next."

"What do you mean 'shift'?" I was beginning to grow nervous, looking around us at the vast emptiness that seemed to draw in closer with every breath.

"Don't you remember? We all agreed to take shifts to keep watch. You're here until dawn—two hours from now," she answered, confused. I could recall none of it, shaking my head in dismay. By the way she sat up and wrapped part of the blanket around me, I could tell she noticed. Sighing, she whispered, "What's another two hours?"

# TWELVE

Dawn couldn't come soon enough. Even with the quiet and distant company that Heather provided, it had to have been the loneliest and most agonizing night of my entire life. Between losing huge swathes of my memory of prior events I had seemingly been a part of and waiting for the creature to slink out of the darkness to finally put an end to me, I felt as though I had aged a decade at least by the time the first hints of the early morning sun began peering over the horizon. A deep sense of foreboding washed over me as the sky warmed into a vibrant, reddish-pink hue. No birdsong graced us that morning—only the ominous howl of the wind through the trees. It was almost as though the world had died around us, and we were the last living creatures on Earth.

Both Heather and I were visibly exhausted, the hours of silence between the two of us having taken a massive toll on our bodies. Still, she proceeded to stand and stretch, giving me the rest of the blanket as she did so, and began to wake the others, who were all clustered around the other side of the fire pit in a loose pile of bodies. Slowly, I watched them sit up, completely dazed and unaware of their surroundings—like they had just woken up from a bad dream and expected to find that everything they experienced was back to the way it was, only for that wisp of hope to be dashed as they remembered. The nightmare is very much still real.

The air was crisp—far cooler than it should be for this time of year, the bite it carried all but screamed autumn despite still being months away at this point. In that moment, I felt more sadness than dread for the first time since the others started to vanish. *I don't think I'm going to see another Fall. It was always our favorite season.* I pushed the thoughts away, willing myself to continue pushing for survival at all costs—I still had the others. It might take them first.

"We are dangerously low on food and water. Most of the supplies we had left are back at the church," Chuck said to Heather as she was assessing the same rocky overhand from yesterday, likely determining the chance we would be able to scale the Crag this morning. She did not immediately acknowledge the older Washburn, which made him huff loudly in apparent frustration. Without turning to face him, she shook her head.

"No, you can't go back to get anything. Besides, I doubt you even remember the way."

"But you do. We cannot go forward without everything we had. We'll starve to death up there if help doesn't arrive almost immediately," he retorted angrily. She continued to face away from him.

"Are you suggesting we all risk our lives to go back to the last place we saw that thing for what amounts to no more than one additional day's worth of food that was almost definitely picked over by raccoons last night?"

It was then that she turned to look at him incredulously.

By now, Jakob was standing to the right of his older brother in some sort of attempt to coerce Heather into changing her mind. Seeing this, I beckoned Harvey over as we stood behind her. Realizing they were outnumbered, the Washburns backed down with glaring eyes.

"Are our chances looking any better today, Heather?" Harvey asked, his voice notably higher than normal. Despite all of the events of the last few days, this was the first time I thought I heard nervousness in his expression. She nodded.

"I don't think it is going to get any better than this, and I definitely do not want to risk another night down here..." She paused and leaned in. "Especially with how those two are starting to act," she finished, whispering quietly. I could feel their eyes burning into the back of my neck as we stood there—a searing anger that bordered on hatred. It seemed, to them at least, that there was simply no other way than their own, and the survival and safety of the others be damned.

---

Fortunately for us, there was very little to pack as we prepared to resume our trek to the Crag, but the tense quiet drew out what would've otherwise been a swift journey as we closed in on the steeper slopes within an hour of breaking down camp. By now, the crimson sky had dulled, but the sinister energy remained as a constant reminder of the forces that threatened us and their otherworldly, untouchable power.

Despite the sun being fully out and beyond the horizon by now, the forest seemed to cling to the darkness like a blanket, the shadows hiding much beyond our immediate vicinity. Even without seeing it, I knew it was out there somewhere, watching us and waiting for its perfect moment to strike. On occasion, the gentle breeze carried with it the putrid scent of decay no matter which direction it seemed to emanate from.

The beginning of the ascent was slow as we followed Heather around the base, searching for a point at which to climb. After finding such a suitable location, she gave a brief albeit informative explanation of what we needed to know about the Crag and what to avoid in order to not kill ourselves. She stressed the importance of moving slowly and always keeping at least three points of contact on the mountain at all times to minimize the risk of falling. After her lesson, she beckoned to the two Washburn brothers to go ahead, followed by Harvey and myself, with her taking up the rear in order to keep a trained eye on everyone.

I could tell she was incredibly anxious, and I am sure the others could too, but we all were at this point, and there was really no aim in attempting to conceal it. She and I stood together as we watched them commence the climb, swaying back and forth nervously. It left me wondering if there was anything she chose to withhold from her story yesterday, but I found no sense in trying to force the rest of it out of her. We were all spent as it was, and the last thing that was needed was another reason for infighting. After Harvey began his ascent, she slowly opened her mouth and glanced up at me, carefully choosing her next words, almost as though she had indeed spent this whole time planning.

"Sam…"

"Yeah?"

"I can't tell the others, but I don't think we are all going to make it out of this," she said hesitantly. Deep down, I knew that to already be true—yet the nature of this revelation from arguably the most valiant member of the group rocked me to my core. *Why was she telling me this now?* Squeezing my eyes shut, I shook my head as if to try and dislodge the thought. When I opened them again, the world fell silent, and the chill in the air caused the hairs on my arms to stand on their ends. Peering out from around a great pine trunk, I saw the same skeletal face of the creature, its gaping maw of a mouth—smiling. Before I had any chance to react, Heather placed a weak hand on my shoulder, her eyes beginning to well up.

"Do what you can to keep them all alive, Sam. Can you do that for me?"

The words were caught in my throat, and I could not force anything to come out. After a few rapid blinks, the creature was gone—but its presence persisted even in the absence of its corporeal form. I focused back on Heather, who appeared far smaller than before, as if she were being deflated.

"Heather. What's going on?" I asked, trying to conjure up the strength to fight back against the growing panic in my chest.

"I bought you some time."

Blinking again, it was back—its body still and unwavering, like a statue—though much closer this time and fully within view. The air somehow grew even colder and heavier to an almost suffocating degree. In that moment, I forgot about the others, and I wasn't entirely sure that they were even still there. Unlike before, its features seemed almost obscured in a black and wispy mist that clung to its frail frame like tendrils of loose cloth. It began clicking its tongue within its cavernous mouth.

"It's going to be okay, Sam. But I need you to go now. Don't look back."

To my surprise, she pulled me into a tight embrace as if to say goodbye. And, almost as quickly as it had happened, she pushed me away with immense force. The world around me began to spin, and I felt as though I were drowning in an invisible lake. Stumbling forward, I collided with the rough, uneven stone face that scaled the side of the Crag. Without any additional thought, my hands dug into the rock and pulled my weight up as I struggled to breathe. Familiar voices surrounded me as I climbed the first few feet—those of the lost members of the group—all chanting for me to keep going.

Suddenly, as if breaching the metaphysical surface of whatever I found myself drowning in, the world cleared, and the air became breathable once more. Letting out a sigh of relief, my eyes cautiously returned to the ground, perhaps twenty or so feet below. In the small, sunlit clearing stood Heather—a reassuring half-smile on her face—the creature nowhere to be seen now. But before I had any further chance to react, a rush of shadow—almost mimicking a great, black wave—washed the area and vanished nearly as quickly as it had appeared. My heart sank.

Heather was gone.

FOR WHAT FELT like many agonizing hours, I stared in disbelief at the empty clearing below, completely unsure how to even begin processing what had just happened. It was as though she was simply erased from existence in the near blink of an eye—a fleeting memory in a tumultuous story whose end might be closer than expected. I couldn't even begin to comprehend what she had meant by "I bought you some time" and what the implications were for the rest of us. *Were we safe now? Did she somehow sacrifice herself to this thing as a way to appease its ravaging hunger?* The thoughts were flying through my head at a million miles an hour. But the only thing I could convince myself of now was to continue climbing and hope that the others had not yet noticed.

It was much easier to get my mind off of Heather's disappearance while focusing my efforts strictly on the sheer rock face and the placement of my appendages. Having previously been an avid Boy Scout, climbs like this would've been exhilarating to me. It brought me back to the outdoor adventures I used to take with my father when I was growing up. Granted, none of them were nearly as ill-prepared and dangerous as what I was attempting at the moment—completely disregarding the added threat of some supernatural entity that was hell-bent on doing us all in.

My past excursions were often tandem hikes between the two of us—full of switchbacks and iron rungs carefully placed in precipitous mountainsides. As I grew older, the level of the climbs would increase. We'd start rappelling to get my teenage self comfortable with managing a line and the heights. He always instilled a greater fear in me of the fall, but so long as I respected the craft and took my time, I had nothing to be afraid of.

During one incident that anyone could've seen coming on my sixteenth birthday, I had gotten a little too arrogant for my own good and was quickly humbled when my grip failed and caused me to plummet at least a dozen or so feet before my slick carabiner caught on and lurched me to a halt, dangling at least a hundred feet off the ground. My father, ever the pragmatist, simply looked down at me and shouted, "I hope this taught you what I never could. Now, pick yourself up and get back at it. The show ain't over yet."

How I wished he were here with me now, his warm yet

firm presence would at least be comforting in a time like this—it would make me feel safe. But I was all alone. Even with the others, the reality of the situation we all found ourselves in seemed to dictate that all hope had been lost, and we were just too naive to have seen it until now. We were all dead the moment we lost Harlan—we just didn't know it yet.

Despite refraining from taking my eyes off of the wall in front of me, I could tell that the others were somewhere above—perhaps fifty feet or less. I'd likely be gaining on them if I was the only other person with this sort of climbing experience. They would occasionally let out exasperated cries, and a tumble of loose stone would sail past my body as they disappeared into the trees below. I wondered if I'd see one of them fall next, trying desperately to catch themselves as they plummeted only to lock eyes with me one last time—a solemn acknowledgment shared between us. I shook my head. *You are distracting yourself, Sam. Get it together. Heather was counting on you. Don't let her death mean nothing.*

I didn't even know if she was dead or if any of the others were, for that matter. For all I knew, they could be holed up in some cave somewhere—perhaps the place where Harlan buried his fortune like some sort of drug-dealing pirate. *What if this is all some sort of drug-induced psychosis, and we're all part of some elaborate ploy to fake his death?* The thoughts kept the barrage up, subjecting me to countless conflicting ideas that might help explain what was happening to us. I had never been much of a believer in the paranormal, even though the death of Maria had me begging to be wrong. I sought dozens of so-called psychics and mediums to try and find some way to talk to her again but had given up with the mountain of evidence against the practices. She was gone, and I knew there was no way back—no way to commune with the dead.

"Occam's Razor... The explanation with the fewest assumptions about a given situation is usually the most likely to be correct," I whispered to myself under weighted breathing. *There is no rational explanation for any of this—you are fighting something beyond comprehension, and attempting to pit logic and reason against what you've seen will only distract you and kill you. You can't let it win.*

The sweat coating my tiring fingers made it difficult to maintain my grip. Knowing I needed to take a break, I searched for a place to steady myself with the least amount of effort possible. The respite came in the form of a small ledge a few feet to my right, the edge wrapping around into a shaded overhang somewhere out of view. Without thinking any further, I drew closer and pulled my body up onto the flat surface.

It was no more than a foot wide at its best—barely enough room to sit without feeling like I might fall off with my dead legs hanging weightlessly in the air. I scooted the rest of the way to the overhang, dragging my rear through the loose stones and dirt that covered the ledge's surface. Searching through my pack, my heart nearly leaped from my chest as it slipped, the bright yellow flare gun sliding from within. With sweaty hands, I caught it as it nearly toppled over the edge.

*When did this get in here?* I thought to myself, trying to calm my shaking hands. It was returned to my pack, finding a new home in a pocket that had a set of independent metal buckles for an extra level of security. This had to have been planned by Heather in some way—she must've slipped it into my pack while I was drifting last night. *She knew she wasn't going to survive and gave it to me after making what-*

*ever deal she did.* None of it really made much sense to me still, but it was the only thing I really had any sort of explanation for at this point. *Whatever she did, I hope it works, and I hope that I don't fail her.*

---

I WASN'T sure how long I waited there, but it didn't feel like it really mattered—we were either cornered or safe, and there was really no way to tell. There was solace to be had in taking in the surrounding forest so far below, the swaying tops of the pines undulating like waves on a great, green sea. From here, I could almost make out the path we had been following with the lake basin to my far left and the pass that we traced through the ridges and valleys into the old town whose clearing was perhaps only a handful of miles to my front. It felt so much smaller up here—that our trial was insignificant in the context of everything surrounding us. I couldn't decide if this conclusion brought me any comfort or just belittled the grave threat we had been facing that undoubtedly cost the lives of people we knew—people we trusted.

Realizing now that the others were likely much further ahead on their climb than I was, I returned to my work, attempting to make up for the lost time. Much to my surprise, the rest of the group had found a similar ledge to rest on about one hundred feet further up the Crag. They were all extremely exhausted by the looks of their pale, wet faces that seemed to stretch like putty. Harvey was the only one to smile and acknowledge my arrival.

"Hey... where's Heather?" he asked, his tired voice raspy. He reached into his pack and retrieved a metal canister, taking a swig of the liquid contents within. I could hear it slosh and figured that there was not much left of whatever it was.

"She didn't make it... There was nothing I could've done," I responded, defeated. Chuck attempted to get up onto his feet, but his wobbly legs kept him firmly planted on the rock, his tired expression twisting into anger and confusion.

"What do you mean? Did she fall? Where is the flare gun?" He fired off the questions in rapid succession, leaving me very little room to interject before the hysteria started to kick in. I could see the dismay blossoming on each of their faces.

"I have the flare gun. And she didn't fall... *It* took her. I don't know what she did, but she said that she 'bought us some time' or something along those lines."

I collapsed to the ground next to Harvey and slouched against the cliff face, the fatigue I had been ignoring all morning and afternoon washing over my aching body. The group was quiet as they absorbed what I had shared with them, pondering its ambiguity. "Did anyone see her doing anything strange last night?"

"No. She was the first one asleep. We all took turns keeping watch. You two were the last shifts of the night as was agreed on," Chuck replied indifferently. It irked me how little he seemed to care that she was gone—how little he seemed to care that *anyone* was gone beyond their utility to his own survival. His brother nodded in agreement, confirming what the older Washburn had said. I began to understand why Heather might have chosen me over the two of them. *They would sooner let the rest of us die if it meant they could live.*

"What do we do now?" Harvey wondered aloud. It helped to disperse some of the brewing tension in the air, and I think he knew that. *Forever the peacekeeper,* I thought to myself. I envied that of him. Bending over and unclipping the metal clasps to the front pocket of my pack, I retrieved the yellow flare gun from within, confirming that the sole remaining round was still within the chamber.

"I think we are high enough now that this might get someone's attention. Does anyone disagree?"

Their faces all stared blankly back at me, almost unnervingly so. After a moment, they began to slowly nod as if the words needed time to unravel within their minds as they processed what was said. With their tentative support, I brought the gun up widely above my head, the barrel extended as far out from us as I could bring it. Dislodging the safety and pulling the trigger, the final flare was jettisoned into the air in a brilliant eruption of smoke and fire. The round burst into a blinding red stream that soared through the sky, undaunted and pulsating. We all watched, mesmerized by its glow as it careened for several long seconds in an arch before dissipating, leaving a trailing, half circle of smoke in the sky that was slowly erased by the gentle breeze.

Somehow, I wasn't sure I felt any better having fired it off—it felt as though this struggle remained fruitless and nothing of significance had changed. It felt as though all remaining hope had just been dashed in a streak of red fire, and I worried that the others might feel the same. It was all so anticlimactic in a way that was difficult to describe. *What if no one saw that? What if no one is coming to save us?* No matter how hard I tried to clear my mind of these thoughts, they clung to me with such a ferocious, iron-tight grip.

It was some time before anyone else in the group spoke, watching the sun slowly reach its pinnacle in the sky before beginning to sink to the west, turning the heavens a beautiful shade of orange and magenta. In another time, I would've considered it breath-taking, but there was simply nothing to feel about it now—it represented another long and dark night with one fewer person to keep us going. It was much to my relief that someone decided to jolt me from my depressing, inward spiral.

"Sam, do you think Heather stopped that thing somehow? Is that what she meant by buying time?" Harvey asked, almost timidly but still hopeful nonetheless.

"I don't know. I wish I did, man. I wish I did..." I sighed. There was no point in lying or trying to skirt around the truth. It was then that Chuck cleared his throat.

"Maybe she worked some ancient magic or something that the Natives do. Sounds about right," he spewed, disdain in his tone. "Regardless of what she did, I think it is only fair that we drink and pay our respects. But I am mostly just looking for a socially acceptable excuse to drink the whiskey I brought..." He trailed off as he became distracted by the pack in front of him, violently rummaging through its contents until he retrieved a large, metallic cylinder, motioning for us to all hand him something to pour into. Slightly disgusted, I passed along my empty canister, my mouth watering at the thought of something to drink.

Unsurprisingly, the liquor was incredibly warm and had begun to leech some of the inner metal lining of the container it was housed in, giving it an almost bloody aftertaste. *Fitting,* I reckoned. This was undoubtedly a terrible idea and had a far greater chance of getting one of us killed than it would ever balance out in the short-term morale boost it might provide. Still, I could not resist the temptation to continue—the dark allure of mental respite and to temporarily numb the pain. I threw the year of steady alcoholism and the challenge of clawing myself out of that pit aside, knowing that there was truly nothing to stop me.

After a while, I had even tricked myself into thinking that we were safe, whether warranted or not. I simply wanted the comfort of feeling like things were even remotely normal again and that I could just return to my life like the events I had lived through were never real—that Harlan would be waiting for me to tell him all of these insane stories at our first appointment back in Pinewood. I needed the assurance that everything was going to be okay.

As the whiskey was consumed, the tension within the group seemed to lift, and all previous animosities towards each other dissipated. While I did not partake, Harvey was busy sharing more sailing stories with the Washburn brothers, who hung on every sentence and laughed like deranged psychopaths at anything that even remotely resembled a joke. They almost seemed human for the first time since we started the hike.

By the time the sun had dipped below the horizon and the darkness of night settled in, even I was finding myself involved in the conversations. The haunting feelings seemed to drift away further and further, allowing me to believe even more that things would be all right in the end. This felt almost like the very first night of the trip as we settled in, telling each other ghost stories with an innocence regarding what was to come. It reminded me of the dauntless human spirit my father always used to tell me about. *I hope this taught you what I never could. Now, pick yourself up and get back at it. The show ain't over yet.*

Just as I was beginning to feel the last vestiges of looming fear fade away, I thought I heard something on the wind. At first, I reckoned it was nothing more than the way the breeze was hitting the jagged edges of the Crag, but it grew louder and clearer with every passing second, swelling like the crescendo of an enigmatic orchestra. Conflicting emotions of dread and excitement coursed through my body. *Was that someone coming to rescue us?* In my drunken stupor, I only considered what might be an attempt at salvation. These were quickly dashed when I could clearly make out what I was hearing. It was a cacophony of different voices shouting in unison, carried hauntingly on the wind.

There was no mistake. It was Harlan, Marcus, and Arnie. And Heather.

# THIRTEEN

At first, I was unsure of if the others could make out the same voices, but my fears were confirmed when I saw the looks on their stark white faces—they could hear it, too. For the next several excruciating minutes, we all sat in total silence, soaking up the dissonant wails of our fallen friends—or perhaps something else—the inky blackness of nightfall cloaking us on the desolate mountainside. We were all alone up here, subjected to the indescribable cries of people we had once known.

They were strained and raspy while also seeming to emanate from nowhere and everywhere at the same time, carried on the wind from somewhere down below in the shadowy pines. For all I knew, they could be down there, alive and calling out for us to find them. The human in me—and, to some extent, the whiskey—wanted to climb back down to help them. But the eerie, subconscious voice that quietly whispered in the back of my mind and caused the hairs on the nape of my neck to stand on end told me those were not the voices of my friends. Something was off about them.

It wasn't until I could clearly make out what they were saying that I heeded those warnings. *"Nowhere to run, nowhere to hide,"* repeated over and over again. By now, the whiskey that had previously worked its magic to relieve my tension was actively working against me and forcing me into a cage with my thoughts. *It's using them... It stole their voices.* I wanted to scream—to let out something, anything—but nothing would come. Only the madness I had been staving off for so long.

"Think that's actually them?" Harvey asked, his voice just above a whisper. It was difficult to tell in the near pitch black we all found ourselves in, but I heard the Washburn brothers shift, the loose stone and dirt beneath their bodies crunching audibly. I only assumed they were turning to face the direction Harvey's voice had come from.

"There is zero doubt in my mind that—whatever *that* is—is not them," Chuck said, oddly composed given the circumstances.

"It's got to be the creature, then, right?" Harvey returned. "Do you think it's trying to lure us down?"

"I'm still not entirely convinced those ghost stories are actually true. That's all they are, right? Ghost. *Stories...* Heather was just using some old tale she heard from her parents to try and explain what has been going on—" Chuck started.

"If you're so sure about it, then why have we been seeing this same creature? Why are we hearing people we can only presume are dead? If you're going to act so smart and put together to convince yourself that you know what is going on when you are just as afraid as the rest of us, why don't you tell us what it is?" I interrupted, finally breaking through the mental anguish I had been trapped in. By the way that Chuck huffed and then fell completely silent after,

I knew that my hit had landed squarely where I needed it to. "Heather's final wish to me was to make sure I got everyone out, and I *will* be damned if I don't try. Now, for that to happen, we all need to be on the same page from here on out. That means no more ignoring the elephant in the room... What we are up against is not explainable. I don't think there is a single scientific thing that will tell us what is going on. The only thing we've got is our basic senses, right? And what are we being told right now? It can't reach us up here."

"How do you know that?" Jakob scoffed.

"If it could reach us, why would it be wasting time trying to lure us back down? If even one part of Heather's story is true, it must be that this place had some significance and that, *maybe*, this is land it is not allowed on," I reasoned, trying to convince myself of what I was saying at the same time.

"Why would she seemingly sacrifice herself right before reaching somewhere safe then? I hate to play Devil's Advocate, but I'm not about to place all of my bets—and my life—on something like this," Chuck retorted.

"And maybe it still can. I'm just as lost on all of this as you are, man. Maybe she didn't know. It's not like this didn't take place hundreds of years ago and was a word-of-mouth story. But we don't have many other options right now."

This seemed to resonate with the others more, as there were no further objections.

"What if we didn't sleep?" Harvey asked, unprovoked. And, as if on command, the haunting wails of the not-friends fell silent, leaving only the subtle howl of the wind against the carapace.

"What has that got to do with anything?" Chuck challenged, bewildered.

"Well, I can't speak for you, but it seems like it appears more when you're dreaming, right? What if sleeping lets it get closer to you somehow?"

"No, wait, I think Harvey is on to something here," I responded, connecting threads I hadn't realized were dangling in front of me this whole time. Despite not being able to see it myself, I could tell that he was smiling back at me. "If the only place we had seen it previously was in our dreams, who's to say that by not sleeping, we won't be taking away from its powers or something?"

Chuck simply started laughing, a drunk, hysterical, grating kind of laughter that was equal parts insulting.

"You've both officially lost it! This is insane. This is *actually* insane."

Based on the way his faint silhouette moved, I could tell he was taking another drink from the canister of whiskey while he paused to formulate his next words. "I think this obviously means that neither of you is fit to see this through to the end, especially you, Sam. If I didn't know any better, I'd say you're verging on or wholly in the throes of a full-on, psychotic breakdown. I'm not a doctor, but I don't think it would take one to see it. You are mad!"

He continued laughing, though this time, I knew it was solely directed at me. I could feel the heat of the rage burning within slowly start to claw its way up from the pit of my stomach and pool in my head, scorching its way down my arms until my fingertips were tingling. I dug them into the cool mixture of dirt and rocks beneath me, fighting the white-hot malice within. *Nobody has to know. Harvey wouldn't tell.*

It wasn't until the thoughts had flashed across my mind that I realized the awfulness of the things I was seriously contemplating in that instant. Never once had I found myself so close to justifying the death of another person, yet this was the second occurrence in just a few short days. *Perhaps the creature was somehow influencing me—playing mind games of some type to get its way?* There was really no way to ever confirm.

---

I DID NOT SPEAK to either of the Washburn brothers for the remainder of the night, though I could still hear them in the dark somewhere further down the ledge, continuing to drink. Harvey had joined me, leaning against the cliff face, waiting for the first light of the new day. We had spent some time talking, reminiscing on our lives prior to all of the events that had transpired. I learned of the names he and his wife had considered for their unborn child—a bittersweet exchange as I could tell he wasn't convinced he'd live long enough to see it through. I thought he'd make a good parent and said as such. Half as a joke, but undoubtedly still serious at the roots—he proposed that I be the godfather, to which I accepted immediately.

The discussion eventually transitioned to that of a plan. We both knew that the Washburn brothers could not be trusted and that their goal would be to survive at any cost necessary, even if it meant the unfortunate sacrifice of anyone else. There was a renewed warmth and confidence in myself, knowing that, despite everything that had happened and every reason to feel otherwise, Harvey still had my back through it all. After assessing what little we had left for supplies, we determined that we'd only have another day of food and water between the two of us—and that was likely reflected with the others. Chuck was ultimately right—we really needed those supplies left behind in the church.

---

Another day and night had come and gone with us still clinging to the side of the Crag, waiting to be saved—or killed. As expected, our supplies were completely diminished, even with extensive rationing. You can only stretch a handful of trail mix and granola so far, and a gulp of water doesn't last very long against the heat of the late summer sun. I knew that if we stayed up here, exposed to the elements, for any longer and without supplies, we would surely die. At this point, I was convinced that no help would be coming and that we needed to act fast before the onset of delirium.

Scanning the verdant, green horizon, my gaze fell upon a deep gash somewhere to the southwest. It was growing more difficult to concentrate, but I assumed it was no more than ten or so miles away in a straight line. *Could that be the river we crossed coming in?* I thought to myself, trying to focus back on the first day of the trek, attempting to cross-reference the first time I saw the Crag. *It had to be the river.* Nudging Harvey, I pointed loosely in that direction.

"Think that could be the river we crossed coming in?" I asked, my voice growing tired and raspy. He squinted hard, placing a palmed hand flat above his brow to shade against the beating of the sun. After a moment, he hesitantly nodded.

"It very well could be, I suppose."

"So if we just head that direction, we could be back across it and find our way home!" I exclaimed, feeling a sudden rush of energy I didn't know I still had reserved.

Harvey shrugged, mulling it over, slowly beginning to smile. "We can even see what supplies are left in the church on our way. I'm willing to bet we could follow that railroad most of the way to the edge of the river!"

"That sounds as good a plan as any. Count me in!" he boomed, a new-found galvanization in his vibrant voice. Unsurprisingly, the excitement drew in the interest of the Washburns, who had previously secluded themselves to the other side of the ledge that wrapped around a sharp corner of the cliffside. Their eyes were wide and bloodshot, with dark bags resting below them.

"What are you two talking about now?" Chuck prodded weakly.

"We have an idea. See that over there? That's got to be the river we crossed coming in. Now if we just climb down, we can stop at the church to get what's left of our supplies and make it there by nightfa—"

"Drop it. We signaled for help. If we leave now, we might get lost again and miss our shot. Ghost or no ghost, we are not going back down there without a means of defense," he growled. Despite his ailing features and weakened state, Chuck looked not too dissimilar to a rabid animal, cornered and ready to put up a fight.

"And we don't want to wait up here to die! We will leave on our own if we have to," I retorted, seeking the advantage. I could feel Harvey's massive body standing close behind me. Undeterred, Chuck continued.

"We're not going to let you leave with half of the supplies."

"What supplies? We are spent, Chuck. There is nothing left!" Harvey shouted back viciously. Even I was startled by the tone in his voice, but it resulted in Chuck and Jakob slinking backward a few steps. Seeing an opportunity, I reached out and took hold of the pack they had been guarding and tossed it over my shoulder to Harvey, the contents rattling within.

"We're leaving with this. I suggest you follow," I said coldly. At first, neither of them responded, choosing to glare instead, hatred burning in their eyes. Whether they decided to join us or not was entirely up to them. Part of me hoped that they wouldn't, but another part, much deeper down, hoped that they would. Taking what little remained of their supplies would surely doom them if help did not arrive in time—if ever. But it could also act as a motivator to two otherwise stubborn men. These sentiments were quickly thrashed.

"Killing us just like his wife," Jakob muttered under his breath to his older brother. It was like a switch flipped. Suddenly, the world seemed to slow down to a near halt as my heartbeat quickened. *What did he just say...* It was as though I could not process the words that spewed from his mouth, yet they came so clearly all the same. My blood began to boil, and the same malice I fought to contain for so long returned in a searing fury.

Within seconds, I was on top of Jakob—taking him completely by surprise. He didn't have a chance to react as he toppled to the ground. The world around us faded into the background as I repeatedly bashed his skull against the hard stone beneath us, this head ricocheting like a ball on pavement with each consecutive blow. I could see the fear in his wide eyes, but I could not stop—not that I even remotely wanted to.

When he started trying to fight back, I reached up and punched him square in the face, likely breaking his nose with the slug, blood immediately pouring from his nostrils. I could feel someone, likely his brother, trying to pull me away, but they could not dislodge me, no matter how hard they worked. Jakob was my only focus, and I would see this through to the end this time.

The harder I pressed my attack, the less resistance he managed to put up, likely losing consciousness in the process. Yet I continued to pummel his body until his face was horribly swollen and disfigured. There was someone shouting at me in the background, their voice distant and echoing endlessly. More frantic attempts to pull me away, more failures. I knew what needed to be done. Sliding his limp, broken body toward the edge of the overhang, I rolled him over the edge, watching him flop and vanish into the trees below. I felt a rush of warmth wash over me that seemed to evaporate nearly as quickly as it came, a fitting climax and conclusion to a primal rage that had been simmering since even before the start of the trip.

*Did I really just do that?* The thought repeated in my brain, cycling through an endless feedback loop as the vision of what just transpired flooded my head. It was like a blindfold had just been lifted from my eyes, and the sounds of the world around me returned with thunderous force. It had been Harvey who was shouting at me during the whole ordeal.

"Sam! Sam! Oh God... We have to go... We have to go, Sam!"

When I stood up, my legs felt wobbly underneath my weight, nearly causing me to take the same fall Jakob had moments prior. Turning around, I saw Chuck's limp body slouched against the cliff face, blood pooling near his head. Evidently, I had knocked him off his balance while he was trying to save his brother, likely causing him to hit his head on one of the many jagged rocks strewn about the surface of the ledge. I could not tell if he was still breathing or not, but part of me did not care either. *He deserved it all the same.*

"We can't tell anyone else about this, Harvey. You understand me?" I asked, trying my best to keep my cool. He nodded sheepishly. "Come on, we need to get moving. We have to make it to the river by nightfall."

---

We followed a series of narrow crevices and natural switchbacks in a different direction down from the ledge, spurts of free-climbing added into the mix where needed. Not a single word was spoken in the near two hours it took to return to the forest floor. I think we both knew that there was no going back now—the irreversible had already been done. Suddenly, the surrounding trees and underbrush were foreign and hostile, with shadowy secrets hidden deep within its sprawling reaches. I wondered if we might stumble across the mangled and broken remains of Jakob somewhere down here, but I let the thought slide away. *There's no going back now.*

We followed the base of the Crag to the right for some time, finally returning to the haunting location where we had begun our ascent nearly two days prior—the same place where I had watched Heather disappear without a trace in a wave of inky darkness. I shuddered at the recollection of it, how chilling and silent it had been. There would have been nothing in the world that could've prepared me for the eeriness of it only to return to it. I tried not to remember the pained look on her face or imagine what her final thoughts might have been. Checking the dim sun peaking through the treetops and the growing layer of thick, gray clouds, I reoriented our direction so that we were facing back toward the old village and the river—our ticket home. Pushing the detrimental thoughts crowding my mind aside, I focused on the task at hand and our way to salvation. Beckoning to Harvey, we hurriedly retraced our steps, winding through the trunks of towering pines that loomed overhead, judging.

It wasn't long before we were standing at the perimeter of the rotten village and the dilapidated church, which appeared to list to the side even more so now than the last time I had seen it. The back door we had made our hasty exit from remained ajar, the hinges barely retaining its soggy fixture to the rest of the structure. Through the opening, we could only see a wall of pure darkness—a shadow so dense, it was only comparable to the blackness at the bottom of the ocean.

"Sam... I don't think we should go back in there," Harvey whispered, his voice unfamiliar after being quiet for so long. I could hear the unease in the tone and, deep down, knew that I agreed. *But the supplies. We don't know how long it will take to get back once we find a way to cross the river, and those supplies could keep us going for another day or two.* I nodded for a few seconds before shaking my head, shuffling the clouding thoughts away.

"The stuff that is left in there could be the difference between us making it back and dying out here. You want to see your wife again? You want to be a father? This might be the only way," I explained, ignoring the harshness in my words. *Something is wrong with me.* Harvey was left staring blankly at me for a moment, his eyes darting back and forth as if waiting for me to say something else, something favorable—something that the Sam he had known before would've said. The agony and anguish I felt when he muttered a simple "okay" would undoubtedly haunt my memories for years to come. In lock-step, we entered back into the church.

It took several long seconds for my eyes to adjust to the darkness within. Through the broken glass in the windows, I could not make out the village beyond or the sun that should've been proudly shining overhead. It was like we were cast into some forbidden and depraved realm, unable to be redeemed by the light we hid from. The musty air in here was cold, reminding me more of the depths of a cave with each passing breath.

We spent very little time recollecting or investigating the unearthly and unholy nature of the confines of this place, instead focusing on sifting through the remnants of our supplies, surprisingly untouched by anything in the last three days. I tried to avoid thinking about it, but there were simply too many questions. *Surely, a raccoon or two would've found this stuff by now. What stopped them from finding it?* I asked myself despite already knowing what the answer must be.

With the supplies scavenged and the items of use stored safely away in our packs, I tossed a glance over to my sleeping bag still rolled out in the corner, its vibrant orange exterior seeming to shimmer, calling out to me. It was as if it was the only thing in the whole space that had any semblance of light to it. Drawn in like a moth to a flame, I encroached on its place of rest as if I were disturbing it. As I began to try and roll it back up, my heart stopped. There was something—or someone—zipped inside, their unmoving and cold mass practically begging to be left alone. But my innate inhibitions could not stop me. I had to know.

With shaking hands, I drew down the metal zipper from the very top of the bag, the mechanism clattering on the teeth that lined the edge. No movement. I slowly peeled back the top, revealing a horribly beaten and bloated body, the caved and disfigured face being almost unrecognizable. Reeling back, I dry-heaved for a moment, desperately not to lose what little contents of my stomach remained. The stench was foul and quickly engulfed the room. When Harvey heard my coughing and sputtering, he rushed over, pulling me to my feet.

"We got what we needed. Time to go," he muttered, keeping his voice down. It wasn't until we were near the back door again that I pivoted my head around, my gaze returning to the forbidden corner with my sleeping bag. Standing there was the same body I had uncovered, its face seeming to have clawed back time from the decay. It was smiling at me, the sunken, gray, and dead eyes seeming to glint in the low light. There was no doubt in my mind that it was Jakob or what was left of him.

I did not tell Harvey what I saw, not that him knowing would have changed anything anyway. All we could do now was keep moving and put as much distance between us and that church as we could in as short a time as possible. Though, I knew that deep down, I would be seeing that place again and again for the rest of my life. And I would deserve to.

We quickly passed the remnants of the collapsed train station where we had seen the creature once before during the storm, almost catching its echoing silhouette as we went. Soon, the hollow corpses of those ancient wooden structures disappeared into the background as we barreled down the tracks. Overhead and through the tunnel-like canopy of the tree branches, I could see that the clouds were growing darker, taunting us. Another storm was fast approaching.

# FOURTEEN

We had only progressed perhaps another three miles or so when the first distant rumble of thunder rang out from somewhere miles away. It was eerily quiet and foreboding in nature, nothing sudden and direct about it—firmly telling us that it was there and it was coming. Something about this storm, in particular, felt indicative of the situation we found ourselves in and, thus, made it infinitely more dangerous. We never once dared to look back through the tunnel of darkening foliage for fear we might see it lurking in the background—waiting.

The first drops of rain began pelting the backs of our heads a mile later as we approached a junction in the tracks, a set of iron rails and rotting ties veering hard to the right and disappearing around an overflowing bend of dense underbrush and fallen trees. Initially, I had kept my pace, ignoring the additional path, but I stopped a moment later when I realized that Harvey was no longer at my side. Turning around, I saw him hesitantly shifting his weight from side to side, his head rapidly darting between the right and the left paths.

"Harvey! It's got to be this one," I called out, jogging back toward him.

"How do you know?" he asked, unconvinced, when I approached him. The rain was starting to come down heavier now, intermittent flashes of bright light illuminated the sky, quickly followed by the boom of thunder. I knew we couldn't linger for long.

"Just a feeling. You're going to have to trust me," I responded hurriedly. He looked firmly at me, his face darkening.

"Like how Heather trusted you to keep us alive? Like Chuck and Jakob?"

His words stung like a scorching red knife being plunged into my gut, causing me to recoil. At first, I thought I was dreaming, but everything felt too real, too painful—not dull and muted like I was experiencing from underwater. He shook his head, palming his face for a second in his hands. "Sorry. I don't know where that came from."

"We have to keep moving," I responded, placing a reassuring hand on his muscular upper arm and squeezing as tightly as I could manage. And so we continued down the track on the left, passing over an old steel-supported viaduct that bridged the gap of a deep and narrow valley, its bottom cloaked in a murky, gray-green darkness. I checked the time on my watch: 7 PM. *We had to be getting close to the river by now,* I thought to myself.

The bridge seemed to sway and list as the storm front blew in, its winds cascading down the channel of the gorge and ramming against the steel frame. It groaned, protesting the force. Another flash of lightning—another crack of thunder, much, much closer this time. Peering westward, I could see the curtains of rain fast approaching as they poured into the valley. We had to get off of this bridge. Rushing for the other side, a bolt of lightning struck a protruding metal pole about ten yards ahead along the banister on the right. The following crack of thunder felt like it caused an earthquake as the bridge beneath our feet seemed to tremble for several long and agonizing seconds, convincing me it might crumble to dust. However, we reached the other side just as the torrents of rain caught up to us, immediately drenching our clothes and bodies.

It was no more than thirty minutes later that we finally reached the river, the roaring rapids of rising water within reaching the edges of the embankment, frothing and writhing hungrily. The churning waves were black like oil as they lapped at and eroded the dirt along the shores. Within the water, debris consisting of leaves and fallen trees were carried violently to the east on our left.

"Which way now?" Harvey asked, desperately shouting over the roar of the river and the downpour of the rain.

"I think we need to go to the West. Head upstream!" I responded, straining my voice as I tried to match his volume, pointing in an exaggerated manner to our right. He tossed a glance in that direction, his soaked hair plastered to his face, briefly whipping droplets of water as he did so. He yelled something that sounded like agreement, but I didn't wait to confirm.

From somewhere in the dark forest to our right, I began to hear the voices again, and I thought that Harvey did, too, based on the way his body stiffened as we ran. They were shouting angrily, but I could not make out what was being said with any distinction as it was mostly lost in the pounding of the rain on the dirt around us. And, almost as if some enigmatic shroud had been lifted, I could suddenly hear them clearly, chanting, "Nowhere to run, nowhere to hide."

Chills trickled down the length of my spine, and my arms and legs felt numb. The air around us became frigid—a cold so suffocating that I could only imagine it was comparable to being stranded in the middle of Antarctica. The roar of the river became muted and echoing, the sounds of the storm grew distant. *It was here. It would not let us leave.*

"It's coming, Harvey! Keep going!" I attempted to shout, but the words never escaped my mouth as I spoke them. It was like I was crying into a pillow. He turned back to look at me as if to acknowledge what I had tried to say, his mouth ushering out words that I could not hear despite the deafening silence that was growing around us. Despite being unable to effectively communicate, we both understood the dire situation we found ourselves in and picked up the pace accordingly, reaching a near-full sprint.

The rain stung as it pelted my face, and the muscles in my legs were beginning to lock up. Years of physical neglect were beginning to catch up, and I deeply regretted not taking Harlan's previous advice of rekindling my formerly active lifestyle when I first started seeing him. Not that it likely would've worked, even if he was actually a licensed psychiatrist and not a drug trafficker.

I was snapped back to my senses when I saw Harvey's arm shoot up, his hand pointing ahead at something I couldn't quite make out just yet. Squinting my eyes and using my hand to shield them from the rain, I could make it out. *The bridge.* It was swaying in the wind, the middle dipping into the swelling waters that flowed below. A moment later and we were standing at its edge between the two anchoring poles that dug into the dark soil on this side of the river. I turned to face Harvey, smiling, to which he did the same.

The happiness was quickly erased from his face as he

saw something. Before I could react, he pushed me forward, out onto the bridge. After catching my balance, I saw it too. *It.* The creature was tearing toward us from the direction we had just come a moment prior. It let out a guttural and dissonant cry that was a melding of all the voices of those who had died—a cacophony of sorrow.

I moved as quickly as I could manage, stumbling forward and struggling to maintain my balance as I placed my feet in steps along the narrow chord at the bottom of the bridge. The water was rising quickly, perhaps even faster than a second ago. I knew this crossing wouldn't last much longer and hurried my pace.

When I reached the other side, I turned to see that Harvey had only managed to make it about halfway across. His right leg had slipped below the water, and he appeared to be struggling to pull himself back up. The level of the river had risen at least another half foot by now, the current beginning to pull him harder and harder as he dragged the bridge down.

Without thinking, I leaped into action and steadily began my way back toward him. At the quarter-way point, I froze. The creature was standing between the anchors on the other side of the raging river, watching. Its gaunt frame blended in with the dark forest backdrop and the torrential curtains of rain. There was a flash of lightning, and everything slowed to a near crawl, the passage of time seeming to break down as I made eye contact with it. The gaping maw curled into a crooked smile, and it cocked its head to one side.

*You... are... a... coward...* came a voice from within my head, though it was not my own. It was androgynous and ancient, as if emanating from a being older than time itself, clawing viciously at my frail mind. The creature took a step forward onto the bridge, its added weight causing it to dip further into the rapids below. By now, Harvey was up to his mid-torso in the water, fighting and thrashing against the current. His pleading eyes locked with mine, his mouth shouting at me, but I could not hear the words he conjured.

But I was frozen there, unable to think or move. It took another step forward and then another, each one dragging Harvey further into the murky blackness of the river. When it had reached the opposing quarter length of the bridge to my side, there was a crack of lightning and a rush of wind that nearly knocked me off my balance. Without thinking, I bolted back to the safety of the shore, collapsing between the anchor poles to my sides.

When I clambered to my feet and spun around, the creature was only a few feet behind Harvey now—though its gaze remained firmly fixed on me, almost as if it had no interest in him. I paced back and forth for what felt like an eternity, trying to determine what I could do to help him. Deciding I would try again, I stepped back onto the bridge, but my hopes were quickly dashed. It had now surpassed Harvey and was approaching my end. Stumbling backward, I instinctively began to rock the nearest anchor pole to loosen it, the memories of my first nightmare out here returning to haunt me one last time.

The first pole gave way, snapping violently into the water and causing the bridge to list to one side, dislodging Harvey. However, the creature remained fixed to the ropes, unchallenged. I knew what must be done now. I focused my attention on the last anchor until the only thing holding the bridge up was my own strength. I cast one last glance at Harvey, who was staring directly at me, his free arm outstretched toward me. As I let go of the pole, I could finally hear his voice as it echoed around me: "Sam—please."

Both he and the creature disappeared below the surface of the water within seconds in a mass of tangled rope mixing with other debris. I collapsed to my feet as it was washed downriver and vanished into the darkness. Around me, the air grew warmer, and the sounds of the storm returned to a near overwhelming degree. I wasn't sure how long I laid there in the mud, crying, but it could never have been long enough to ever fix what I had just done. *I am a coward. I just killed the only person left in the world that trusted me—that I could call a friend.*

Realizing now that there was nothing more I could do, I stood up and brushed what I could off of my pants and arms, the mud simply smearing on my hands as I did so. I pressed onward, following the outline of the trail through the cloud of rain that nearly obscured the way. Much like in my dreams before, I passed the rocky overhang we had used for shade and rest on the first day, trying hard not to think about the others.

Before long, the trail wound to its conclusion, flowing into the same lot I had been so desperate to see for days now —the haunting silhouettes of the other cars still parked along its edge. I ran up to my truck and nearly tore the door handle off with eager enthusiasm. Climbing inside, I was relieved to have a moment to catch my breath and be out of the rain. *What should I do next? I should go to the police... No. They'd find out what I had done. I need to think. I need to go home...*

With shaking hands, I reached into my soaked pack and dug around the contents until I felt my fingers wrap around a metal key ring. I pulled it out and placed the key into the ignition, turning it over. With luck, the engine roared to life, and the headlights came on, piercing the darkness of the forest in front of it. Throwing the transmission into reverse, I quickly backed out of my haphazard spot, taking one last glance at the line of abandoned vehicles, their dark exteriors reminding me of a parked funeral procession. Only the Washburn truck appeared out of place. As I put them in my rearview mirror, I felt a deep and burning sensation of guilt. *Why me? Why was I the only one to get out? Why do I have to be the one to carry this burden?*

I followed the dark, dirt and gravel road as it wound its way back toward the village of Wendell, my heart racing as I hoped for other signs of life—hoped to feel safe again. But this relief did not come. Despite it being about ten o'clock, the streets of the village were completely deserted, the sole traffic light flashing red and yellow for any passerby that happened along the main road.

Exiting Wendell, I followed Route 40 as it ran along the length of the same river to my right that had claimed the life of Harvey. I began tearing up, brushing them away with the back of my right hand. *I hope it was quick and painless,* though I knew deep down that it was likely the opposite. Drowning would have to have been just about the most agonizing way to die. And at the hands of someone you trusted—who you counted on to keep you going...

I did what I could to keep these dark thoughts at bay, but I knew it would become futile soon enough. If I somehow remained sane after this, it would only be because I became well-acquainted with the bottom of liquor bottles again. Even then, I didn't think that I could carry that weight forever. *I went too deep... They are all dead because of me.* Despite knowing that the only one I had any intention for was Jakob, the deaths of the others felt as though they rested squarely on my shoulders.

By the time that I had reached the base of my driveway, the aging wiper blades could barely keep up with the onslaught of rain pouring down onto my windshield. I gripped the steering wheel with both hands until my knuckles were paper white and felt as though they may burst through my skin. I had to focus—I had to keep my mind off of it.

The truck struggled to make the winding ascent up the side of the hill, deep pockets of mud would occasionally capture a wheel and force me to reverse out. Suddenly, the confines of the cab felt less like a sanctuary and more like a prison cell, the dark pines that lined the drive peering in like spectators. I felt trapped. My heart began pounding in my chest. *What if it was still out there?*

As I rounded the final bend in the drive, my truck accelerated unexpectedly, lurching forward into something heavy, bringing it to a halt just before the dilapidated garage. Stepping out into the rain, I collapsed to my knees before Harvey's motorcycle, the mangled mess of rubber and steel lying partially beneath my front bumper and wheels. Suddenly, I could no longer restrain the torment of my emotions, and I began to weep uncontrollably, digging my fingers into my hair and clasping the locks in firm grips as I pulled hard. This time, I felt every agonizing second of the time I spent there, crying my heart out in the yellow glow of my headlights.

There came another flash of lightning from somewhere above, and I counted the seconds until the clap of thunder, trying to steady my breathing. But it never came. Standing up, I realized I couldn't hear the rain anymore either. The whole world had come to a quiet stop around me. Feeling the hairs on the back of my neck stand up, I raced for the front door of my house, the window panes showing the enveloping darkness beyond. After undoing the deadbolt, I burst inside and slammed it shut behind me, my chest heaving with forceful gasps at the stale air surrounding me.

*Gun... gun. I have to find my gun... Where did I put it? It was in with the stuff Harvey, and I moved to the second room. But then we moved it all to the basement a few days before the trip.* I stared at the door directly in front of me that led below and approached, placing a drenched and muddy hand on the knob. But something stopped me from turning it, something beyond comprehension—something primal. I slowly backed away into the living space, arms outstretched before me. That was when I heard it, a dissonant, bellowing groan that metamorphosed into a roar that shook the house. It was down there already.

Seconds later, the skeletal figure burst through the door as though it were made of paper; its angry and dead eyes affixed to me as though I was the only other thing in the world to it. I dashed to my left, just barely skirting past its lunge. Its haggard body collided with the doorframe of the kitchen with such force that it rattled the contents of the room, even the items still within the many boxes that lined the walls of the space. It let out a guttural growl as it got back up and made another strike, missing only by a few inches this time. I could feel the coldness that seemed to radiate from its form, the stench of decay quickly filling the confines of my house to a near-suffocating degree.

By now, I was backed up against the ancient stove at the far end of the room. Thinking on my feet, I turned each switch over to the maximum level, the natural gas hissing as it erupted from the range, and the smell of rotting eggs permeated the room, overtaking the decay. The creature stood up on its legs and launched itself at me, its talon-like hands outstretched. As I ducked away, a searing pain shot up my spine like a white-hot poker, only to be immediately replaced by an aching cold that seemed to lock up my joints. The pain was indescribable. I knew, instinctively, that it must have got me.

Its body crashed into the stove, ricocheting off of it as though it were rubber. With only a second to think, I knew I needed to get back to the truck. Maybe I could get there before it caught up, and I could escape to town—find an officer or something. But as I made my way for the doorway once more, it grabbed me by the leg, its ice-cold touch locking up my muscles and bringing me to the floor. I kicked as hard as I could backward, catching the heel of my boot squarely in its skeletal face. It merely smiled and flung me against the stairwell at the back of the dining area effortlessly, now standing between me and my only way out. It let out a sound that I could only assume to be a laugh.

Fighting the cold in my leg that almost seemed to creep up from my ankle toward my thigh, I crawled up the stairs, ascending into the hallway above. I knew it would be right behind me. When I reached the final step, I used the railing to pull myself to my feet and braced myself against the wall as I rushed to the very end—my bedroom, its frigid breath on my heels all the while. Slamming the door shut behind me, I rolled over my bed and pushed it against the frame in one fluid motion. I could hear it pounding on it from the other side, the dissonant roars echoing throughout my room. I knew that the door wouldn't hold for much longer—I knew I had no way out now.

In a move of desperation, I placed what little furniture I had on the bed in an attempt to slow down the inevitable. Frantically searching the space for a way out, my eyes stopped on the windows that overlooked the valley. *If I jump, I might be able to crawl to the truck before it notices.*

Without thinking any further, I raced forward, flinging the panes up to the point where I thought they might shatter from the force. Immediately, the wind and rain rushed in, nearly knocking me off my feet.

Before I could lift myself up to the ledge, my heart skipped a beat as the closet door unlatched itself and slowly creaked open. The room was instantly washed in the pleasant smell of fresh lilies, the sounds of everything slowly returning. From within the black confines of the closet, a woman in a white sundress appeared, her flowing brown hair waving in the wind. It was as if the world around me froze, and it was only her and I in this moment.

"Maria?" I stammered, trying to hold back the tears welling up in my eyes. She nodded, a warm smile curling her lips. Melting, I collapsed against the wall, sliding down to the floor, and cried. "I missed you so, so much."

She crouched down next to me, placing a warm hand on my head that seemed to force the cold in my body away. It was as though she had never aged; her face remained exactly the same as the last time I had been fortunate enough to see it. Maria lifted me to my feet and led me to the edge of the bed that was now blocking the door, the sounds of the creature outside constant but distant.

"What are you doing here? Is this real?" I asked, desperately hoping that this was both genuine and not at the same time.

"I am here because you need me," she responded, her voice like silk. It bathed me in a sensation of feelings I hadn't felt since her death over two years ago. I embraced her, holding on tightly.

"What do I do now?"

"You wait," she replied, motioning to the door. Confused, I backed away.

"What does that mean? I have to get away from it. It wasn't supposed to follow me across the river. I thought I would be safe. Heather said I would be safe…"

"It was never going to let you go, Sam. From the instant you crossed that bridge, It was always going to find you. Most people don't see It as early as you do. And most people don't get the chance to see It again and again."

"What do you mean by that?" I asked.

"What you've seen is what everyone will see at the end. You aren't fighting anything more than a representation of time and guilt. For most people, even in my case, I was approached by the same thing that has been haunting you, and It took me with It. It's Death, Sam. And, sooner or later, Death comes for us all."

"So *It's* actually a Reaper?" I couldn't believe the words coming out of my own mouth. *This is insane. I am actually going insane.*

"In a sense, yes. But the weight you allow yourself to carry has only exacerbated Its hunger. Between that and your proximity to such unholy ground, It is essentially rabid. We tried to warn you. Death will not stop until It has claimed what It believes is rightfully deserved. I'm sorry, Sam. You can't go back now. You can never go back in life," she replied, the warmth in her tone almost hiding a sadness buried deep within.

"So you came here to help me *die*?"

"I came here because you don't need to face this alone, Sam. I came here because I love you."

"How can you? I'm responsible for your death. I am responsible for that firefighter's death. I killed Jakob; I may as well have killed his brother. I even killed the only friend I made since you died. I don't deserve any of this. If anything, I should face it alone. I can never forgive myself for what I have done," I cried as she caressed my cheek with her velvet fingers. The Reaper beyond the door grew louder and more restless, pacing back and forth and dragging its claws on the wooden floorboards, frustrated.

"I am not here to judge you based on your actions. Nobody can. The dead don't forgive, Sam, because it is not our responsibility. Only the living can. We cannot change the past—it is merely a part of who we become. Sometimes, it makes us stronger. Other times, it brings us to our knees. But you've always got to pick yourself back up, even if it is the most painful thing you can do. I will always love you, and nothing can ever change that," she expressed, wrapping my hands in hers. There was no point in holding back the tears now. Smiling, I nodded and pulled her back into my arms.

"But how do I know if this is a dream or not? I've had these times where... where I thought I was dreaming, but it was actually real. And the other way around, too! I could wake up, r—right now. How can I know?" I pleaded, burying my face in her neck and sobbing uncontrollably. She reached around, running her gentle hands through my rough hair, squeezing lightly.

"Honey... You don't," she responded softly, caressing my cheek as I pulled away. I stared deeply into her eyes, recalling every intricate detail and drowning in her beauty. Whether it was real or not, I was happy for this moment with her.

"I have missed you so much," I cried, pulling her in for another embrace, squeezing tightly so that I might feel her warmth should this moment be real.

"I missed you too, Sam. I hope this can finally bring you peace," she whispered into my ear, her voice as smooth as silk. I knew then that there was nothing that could keep us apart any longer. Removing the lighter from my back pocket, I flicked the cover open and placed my thumb against the cool, flint wheel. The smell of natural gas had reached its way up to the confines of my room. For the first time in nearly two years, I finally felt as though I was home —my thoughts as clear as the day that would never come. The alarm on my bedside stand began to beep loudly. *5 AM,* I thought. *One more sunrise.*

"Can you stay here, with me, until the end?"

"I never left."

# FIFTEEN

The Pinewood Daily
TUESDAY, AUGUST 13, 1993 — $0.99

ACKERMAN — Firemen responded to a local house fire early Sunday morning along state Route 40 just before the village of Wendell. After several hours fighting the blaze, it was extinguished. Police and investigators were able to assess the cause and determined it to be the result of a natural gas explosion that claimed the life of the homeowner, Samuel H. Stratton, a 32-year-old man who had previously resided in the state of Oregon. He is preceded by his parents, Paul and Helen Stratton, and his late wife, Maria Stratton. He has no other living relatives. A service will be held at the Saint John's Chapel in Ackerman for any friends who wish to attend on Friday, August 16th.

. . .

WENDELL, Riley Bennet, A.P — A local hiking group headed by Dr. Harlan Abernathy was rescued yesterday from near the summit of a mountain thanks to a coordinated effort from state police and the park service, over the span of three days after their trip had become deadly. Details have yet to be fully released to the public as there is still an ongoing investigation into disappearances and deaths connected to the hike. Those rescued include local radio host and meteorologist Chuck Washburn, his brother Jakob Washburn, and Ackerman diner owner Harvey Levett.

EARLY INTERVIEWS with the survivors indicate attacks by wild animals and paranoid psychosis brought on by enhanced sleep deprivation over the course of several days to a week. The source of these attacks has yet to be determined, but locals are already acting, and politicians have been asked for comment.

"(THIS) IS A VERY SERIOUS MATTER, and we will have to address it quickly," said Councilman Keith Reynolds when questioned by our investigative journalists. Insider reports indicate that the county government is considering putting a pause on further development of the local tourism industry until the threat has been assessed and properly neutralized. This comes just months after measures were passed to increase spending on tourism-related programs and grants. There has been no comment from the governor at this time.

. . .

Casualties include, as of the time of this publication, Marcus Brendan, 34, of Pinewood, Arnold Matthews, Jr., 35, of Milton, Heather Prichard, 37, of Pinewood, and Dr. Harlan Abernathy, 51, of Pinewood.

We extend our deepest condolences to the families and friends of the deceased during these difficult times. Service dates and times, and obituaries are to be obtained at a later date.

# EPILOGUE

When I saw the newspaper sitting on the kitchen table, I knew what must be done. Whether it was what he would have wanted or not was not up for consideration—it was the right thing to do. After all, it was what friends were for.

I was incredibly lucky to have a suit in the closet that still fit me despite the many years since I had last worn it—unfortunately, for another funeral. It may not have been the most elegant piece in the world, but it was the best that I could manage on such short notice. The time in the hospital before being discharged would've made it nearly impossible to secure anything else in time.

While getting ready, I was greeted by the tabby cat my wife had brought home a few weeks earlier. He brushed up against my leg, flicking his tail and letting out a whining cry as he did so. "Hungry, Leo?"

He looked up at me and blinked, making a trill-chirp in acknowledgement. I walked out to the kitchen with him following between my legs, nearly tripping me several times in the short trek. Pouring some kibble into an empty bowl near the refrigerator, I knelt down and stroked his back a few times, listening to him purr loudly for a soothing second before returning to the bedroom to finish the task at hand.

With the suit on, I quickly ate a slice of toast and made my way down to the rental car parked out front. It was nothing like my old ride—too many wheels and not enough freedom. It felt confined, safe—an imperfect solution for an imperfect world with a drab interior and sluggish handling. I missed the bike, but I did not want to spend any more time dwelling on it. This sorry excuse for transportation would have to do for now. I climbed in and turned over the ignition, but the engine seemed to struggle to even start.

The drive to the chapel was a short one, but it felt like an eternity. It left me with plenty of time to think about the haunting events of the past few days. I hadn't spoken to either of the Washburn brothers since Sam disappeared in the night with half of the supplies. It wasn't until the following morning that a rescue team had reached us up there on that ledge on the side of the Crag. We were all flown to the Pinewood General Hospital to treat our severe exhaustion and dehydration. I had been questioned by troopers about if I knew the whereabouts of the others that had gone missing. It turned out that they located all of their bodies the next morning in the dilapidated church of a forgotten mining town.

All of it was ruled to be the result of an animal attack, but I'm not sure anyone was convinced of it, especially the Rangers. Their questions, in particular, made it seem as though this was not the first time they encountered such suspicious activity in the wilderness beyond Wendell. Still, they assured us that everything would be alright and that the authorities would handle it. Part of me wondered if I should go back to try and find closure. I pulled myself from my thoughts as I slammed on my brakes, nearly missing my turn.

The parking lot out front was nearly empty, but I still refrained from stopping near the entrance, instead choosing to take a space near the back. From there, I sat for several moments, composing myself. *Do it for him,* I thought. Exiting the car, I somberly made my way to the large oak doors at the front of the chapel and pulled on the large, brass handles that were worn from many years of use.

The interior was dark and musty, the carpet a deep and royal purple that ran the length of the main aisle between several rows of benches. A stained glass window ran from the floor to the ceiling at the back of the main room, depicting some kind of religiously significant person that I did not recognize. Near its base was a closed casket, glinting faintly in the low light. My heart sank, and was almost compelled to run back to my car and leave. But then I noticed that nobody else was here. *Do it for him.*

I slowly made my way down the aisle, passing row upon row of empty benches. Something about it felt even more sad, knowing that I was the only one here. *Surely others would have visited?* As I neared the casket, I noticed that there was one other soul in the building: an older man sitting, nearly hidden, at the far end of the pew on my right at the front of the building, his head lowered as if in prayer. He glanced up when I drew closer.

His face was one I recognized, but I could not put a name to it. I wasn't sure where I had seen him before, he was definitely not a patron of the diner. He appeared tired and worn down from years of hard work, but his eyes were warm and welcoming. With no words exchanged between the two of us, he nodded and smiled slightly, motioning his head to the spot next to him on the bench.

"Glad to see someone else show up for Sam," he said as I sat down to his left. "I was beginning to think I'd be the only one. How'd you know him?"

I chuckled, thinking about the absurdity of the last few weeks. "He started coming to my diner in town. Helped him move some stuff at his house. Lots of old books and familial belongings," I responded, but something began to nag me deep down at the thought of how we came to know each other and how it felt like it related to this strange person.

"It is a shame, really. Sam never made many friends after what happened to Maria. I'm sure he told you about her? Absolutely tragic," the old man said, his gaze returning to the closed casket sitting to our left. He felt distant—as though he wasn't meant to be here.

"Talking about it was how we really got to know each other. I lost someone, and it was devastating. I could never imagine the pain he put himself through. It was hard enough not to blame myself for what happened to them. I'm struggling with it now, if I am being perfectly honest," I shared.

The man turned to me, smiling.

"I can see why he liked you. You're a good man, Harvey. I just hope you can forgive yourself, too. What he did is no indication of who you are. The dead don't forgive, after all. Only you can do that."

*How did he know my name?* Before I could react, he stood up, placing a dark brown fedora on his graying hair, and took his walking stick in hand.

With incredible grace for someone as elderly as he appeared, he slipped past me and made his way toward the casket, placing a frail hand on its black, metallic surface. He whispered something I could not make out and lowered his forehead so that it touched the exterior. *Who is this, and why do I recognize them?* I searched my memories of the nights I spent at Sam's house, sifting through his belongings. It finally came to a rest on a dust-covered photo album where the black and white picture placed into the frame on its front was of the, albeit much younger, man standing next to a woman and a teenage boy, one that might've passed as Sam from another, earlier time.

As the man made his way back up the aisle toward the great oak doors, he turned back around to face me, his smile fading in the dim light. "Remember, the dead don't forgive. And... Harvey? Don't go back to the forest. It's best to let the past rest."

## ABOUT THE AUTHOR

D.C. Picklo grew up in northwestern Pennsylvania. From a young age, he dreamed of becoming an author. After a detour into the world of software engineering, he returned to his passion for crafting intricate and thought-provoking works of fiction. He currently resides in Buffalo, New York with his fiancée and two cats.

Made in United States
North Haven, CT
22 November 2024